WITHDRAWN
UTSA Libraries

By the same author

The Artificial Traveler (1968)

The Mousechildren and the Famous Collector (1970)

In the Animal Kingdom (1971)

Their Family

Their Family

by Warren Fine

Alfred A. Knopf New York 1972

THIS IS A BORZOI BOOK
PUBLISHED BY ALFRED A. KNOPF, INC.

Copyright © 1972 by Warren Fine

All rights reserved under International and Pan-American
Copyright Conventions. Published in the United States by
Alfred A. Knopf, Inc., New York, and simultaneously in
Canada by Random House of Canada Limited, Toronto.
Distributed by Random House, Inc., New York.

ISBN: 0-394-47219-5
Library of Congress Catalog Card Number: 78-171125

Manufactured in the United States of America

FIRST EDITION

LIBRARY
University of Texas
At San Antonio

For Michael Lynch

In a previous volume, *In the Animal Kingdom,* Gerhard Blau, sometimes called Dutch, told of his journey of 1779—to the high, interior plains of this country—with his friends Orcus Berrigan and the Indian woman Sawpootway. At the end, Gerhard's companions went, they said, into the mountains to live; he was prepared to pass through those mountains into country the Spanish had conquered.

I've overheard Gerhard's voice again, telling a story, at some indefinite time, to an unidentified "friend" who may be only his old self, that younger Gerhard Blau who knew Berrigan and Sawpootway in his day-to-day life.

The present story, of 1800–1, issues entirely from Gerhard's imagination, the fiction he invents for two old friends and their imagined children to live in, prompted perhaps by the fear that those he loved might no longer exist.

W.F.

Their Family

I SPEAK TO A FRIEND, MY DOGS LIE
near, and I no longer mind the closing of animals like soft-
est long fingers or petals into the center of a palm or a
flower, animals once so open to me, to my tongue speaking
their names intimately, animals who avert their heads now,
when my bones feel sharp in an intricate relation to my
flesh. Each dog licks himself here with the gentleness of one
who cleans his own wounds, glancing up, almost secretly, as
if I'd wounded him. I see, in this closing of the inhuman
world, another revelation, the emphatic strangeness of my
dogs, the closeness of each animal to his breath, to the
rhythm, of his heart, which almost speaks to me, the male
and female and each dog different in their lying down together, and this awe and difference between us long after the
intimacy of their names.

Now I watch how the names of animals still confirm
themselves, though I've grown wary of fierceness in the closure of the petals and fingers, as the flower becomes the hard,
round fruit, and my hand closes upon the new thing, grip-
ping it, and my teeth nip through the tough skin. I do not
cease to wonder at animals, telling a story to my friend,

who, listening carefully, leans toward me as if out of one dream into another; and it sounds to me as though we both speak in what has become a single voice, so aware of the rhythm of our lungs and hearts, as if our breath and pulse, in expulsion and return, combined to words within our difference, as his silence, listening to me, seems only the alternation of my speech, as if each word knew its shadow; and he is comfortable to me, fulfilling the rhythm of my tale, as though I couldn't breathe without him, or hear my own pulse or voice, after animals closed on themselves.

HIS BODY, IN ITS SLOW LABOR: THE trapper, Legget, arrived at noon; he came in the thaw, ascending from one valley toward another up the gorge. The stream swept past him full of debris, as the mountain, dissolving, seemed to oppose him with its waste. Legget trailed his pack mule behind, his body's progress mule-bound, his animal resistant. The water poured to him around the bend and, above his head, the snowline receded toward the twinned peaks, unveiling the face of the mountain, human or animal features descending while white blood rose into snowy horns, reaching an ultimate pulse in the world he reentered after one year. The ridge-faced mountain —white multiple brows, broken nose, long-mouthed smile—became more familiar to the trapper as he progressed, pulling his pack mule like a burden on his single intention. Sweat dripped from the jaw he'd shaved that morning, as water he'd followed into mountains wound from its source. Soon the bend would become only an outcropping of rock he'd passed beyond, but the mule would still be reluctant behind him, like a reminder of a past or world once even more familiar than the mountain became to him now. In the thinning air, his body strained, as if it would transcend its own pulse—to become a rhythm of white blood in the mountain, his body inclined toward a future he couldn't imagine yet. Legget came, clear of the bend, upon a man.

What the trapper, blond and slender, saw above the bend: was Orcus Berrigan, the father of the girl, waist-deep in the current where the flooding water pooled over old banks, Berrigan, beneath a pine tree, lifting netted trout, his body bent down to the fish, fingers tangled in the web as if in a woman's veil, Berrigan swelling with his catch, becoming full in the brown skins he wears, his head looming larger from gray, raised from the goat-fleece collar. From slender beginnings, he blooms in the relation of sun, tree, fish, and the running pool flooded where he bent half submerged while captured fish spun off, in his hands, distinguished yet elusive colors, as fish mediated reflecting poles of sun and pool, while Berrigan becomes all the scene, combining these things under the pine tree, and the pool seems also to shine, within the surface of the sun, as Berrigan, manipulating fish in the veil, consumes all, as if into the mountain. In his net, the rainbow trout turned about, variety of color, while he straightened his body over the water.

The trapper, unseen yet, saw Berrigan beneath the isolated pine, under the flushed horns of the mountain, those high peaks thawing, their thick sweat swelling down an animal or human face, the rocky earth black all the way down to the water, the mountain unlocking in thaw, white snow on the highest ridges as if bones cut through the brows while, below, black roots of the pine, thick as the mountain's sweat, emerged from black holes like snakes snarled together into the single tree trunk. The mountain's interior opens, pours down the gorge through the figure of Orcus Berrigan. He opens the mountain, in his growth. He rose under the tree, within the brief, rapid pool. The mountain pours through Berrigan, who held fish, and it comes to the blond trapper, whose hair reddened in disintegrating noon. The trapper watched the scene he'd entered with the reluctant mule, while Berrigan increases in the thaw, between tree and mountain, between the sun and the pool.

What the trapper, relaxing, releasing the mule reins, came for was the girl named Dutchess, Berrigan's daughter, who appears, seated high on a pine bough, her hands on a higher bough, her white shift shining while she combs her dark hair with long fingers flared slightly under the nails. Pine needles, spinning, fall down about her, indicating an animal above. When Legget looked above Berrigan and saw her, he saw nothing of her face but the wide, smiling mouth, for that was all he'd seen the one time before, in the summer, when she was distant in the unentered high valley where she lived with her brother, father, and mother.

That previous year he'd seen her from so far away that he'd had to imagine most of her, as she's imagined now in the tree, and he'd taken fear and hurried to the safety of the camp, to other men like himself. He'd approached Berrigan when the father came into the camp of trappers and hunters; but the wife had ruled from the valley, in the Indian language Berrigan translated; it was her word Berrigan brought back to him. Berrigan had said to try again some time later.

Now Legget came again. When he saw her, in this

vision, her brother enters, disturbing the cones and needles as he climbs into the boughs above his father's head. Legget identified the brother by the long and smiling mouth, that is like hers, and he remembered he'd seen the brother close in last year's camp, with his father, and through the young man's features, he imagined the twin sister. So, as young Dutch climbs toward his sister, the two were paired in Legget's mind, so one child of Berrigan couldn't be conceived without the other; Dutchess couldn't exist without the physical, visible presence, in Legget's world, of Dutch. Legget's head swam under the vision, of siblings in the lodge-pole pine that didn't seem to him his own vision, but one he participated in, as though, after entering mountains, he'd entered the imagination of another man. Dutch climbs, flared fingers and body, dissolving like hers at the edges, and he disturbs Legget's hopes for success, ascending with the grace of a serpent, from the tree's dark root-holes, to sit beside his sister on her bough and spread his fingers in her dark hair. Sister and brother gaze above, through falling green needles. Then the animal above them becomes apparent, audible, an orange-red cock in the thinnest branches, crowing their union, mocking Legget's desire, this trapper driven long before to rocky mountains—rocks once blue to him in the distance as he rode up from the plains—into this love and this sudden vision of cock and siblings; for Legget had been cast out by his stepmother who, folding his father in her white arms, had expelled him from the home he'd known, Legget fleeing then to his mother's sunken grave, where he'd pleaded for her help.

During memory, cock and siblings disappeared from the tree, fled while he'd stood alone by the old grave, wishing his mother up into air. Far now, from that pleading with death, Legget studied black holes, where tree roots of the lodge-pole pine arose or descended, holes like places he might have come from; as Orcus Berrigan shouldered the fish and saw him, over the water. Looking up, Legget greeted the other man, who seemed, at first, too surprised to speak.

BERRIGAN ASKED, AFTER MOVING ONE hand before his face, why Legget had come again. He spoke as if that wasn't what he'd meant to say to the trapper.

Legget said he'd come to wed her. He said he meant Dutchess, in the valley. He stared at the mountain above the fisherman; the rock seemed his own face aged to mock him, his elder voice's echo, as if he aged in sound thrown and returned across the water while the mountain concealed the valley where the girl lived sheltered. His own face struggled not to reveal her, through tears, as his secret. He asked if Berrigan was against him now.

Berrigan said he was no more against him than last year, no more than last summer, no more than he'd been.

Legget risked a glance at the treetop, hoping; but the girl had gone, the boy had gone and the cock had. Those images had been removed from Legget. He asked if Dutchess, Berrigan's daughter, was well.

Berrigan said they all were.

Legget would come see for himself, he said.

Berrigan said no, he wouldn't while the woman opposed him. The fish lay out of Legget's sight, down Berrigan's back in the net flung over his shoulder.

Legget said he asked to look at her only for a moment, to see her *close,* to speak to her only for a moment; that was all. But Berrigan's stance was like the language of the mother's opposition. The fisherman scarcely moved, only readjusting the net full of trout; but he seemed about to depart from the water. Legget said this time he would come to her, no matter what opposed him; he was determined. He saw Berrigan, as if in departure, readjusting the net on his other shoulder while he said, and repeated, that Legget wouldn't come without consent.

Berrigan floats, in agreement with Legget's will and imagination, belly up in the pool. Fish pour down within the net that covers Berrigan's body; those long fish cover his sides like scales. Legget heard the other's heavy sighs. The pack mule, transposed, in imagination, to the other shore, pulls a rope that's tied around the floating man, and turned around the rough fulcrum of the lodge-pole pine, while Legget saw himself: he sits astride the girl's father and arches through the pool's current. Berrigan is a ferry the mule pulls into shore. The mule strains with his burden, his stiff hairs filled with sweat, and the taut rope cuts the tree's bark.

Legget asked why Berrigan was against him. The floating image of Berrigan faded.

Berrigan said he didn't know Legget, that he'd only met him a few times, that he knew Legget to speak to; but his woman, Sawpootway, had said, as Legget knew, that she knew him well, too well for her ease, too well to let him come to their daughter. Berrigan said the trapper was a terror from her past, too much a reminder of old death; she mistook him for someone else.

They were silent while Berrigan considered Legget,

secretly, as if himself guilty of some old, serious sin, afraid Legget would catch him watching; but Legget saw the look, and Berrigan said, quickly, but with the emphasis of something important, that Legget was nearer his own age than near the age of his daughter and son. Then he said he'd speak to the woman if Legget would wait there, to tell her Legget had come again.

Berrigan studied Legget; a background of mountains beyond the trapper; and thought of an invisible valley, not his own, below the bend. Berrigan felt mostly the coldness of water rushing through his thighs and around his belly in white foam, the pressure of the river against him, as his genitals wrinkled against his belly, penis and testicles tightened and risen, as far as they could go. He saw his son and his daughter running with the hounds in the valley, while Sawpootway watches, mending, on her porch. The woman's mouth is closed, but she opens her eyes. She sees Berrigan come down toward her with fish. Berrigan, standing in water before Legget, saw her and he saw his children play. He waves down, and the hounds turn toward him—Hasty, Cinco, Pride, and Spook—their long noses lifted toward the man who'll come down among them.

Legget said he would make his camp there.

Berrigan had forgotten the trapper's presence, lost in someone else's vision, or he'd been consumed in imagination in a future event. He said he'd return in the morning; he turned his back, the fish hung down, and he went toward the land, while water troubled his body. The pool had been cold as the sun was hot. Legget diminished in him, falling vague even in contrast to liquids and gases, and to the fish slung down

Berrigan's back, as if the connection between the two men was unreal, as if they didn't remind each other of something else, something of value.

Under the pine tree, near the dark roots, Berrigan stepped from the pool; the waterline receded down him, skin-covered feet clear at last, as he lunged up the incline. Berrigan's strength had been natural in water, like an elephant's, ponderous and sure with grace. He let the trout dangle at his side, in their webbing, while he turned back toward Legget. He said here was food, for the time the trapper waited.

One by one, Berrigan threw four reflecting fish over the pool, his trout through thin air dividing the sunlight and water; the fish cut through the scene; they continued the rhythm of Berrigan's arms. Orcus Berrigan, like the thawing mountain, contained his family. He lifted each trout, singly, like a messenger, a gentle arc of fish, in invitation. Each lofted fish achieved, between the men, a freedom and repose of flight, each ferried trout softly cleaved the interval, contaminating their slow bodies, revolving on axes, threaded between men, as though both sun and pool thawed into the May air, to become the medium trout naturally breathed in, as if men's bodies thawed for the fish, throwing or catching—Berrigan's hands outgoing, releasing his catch; Legget's hands gathering into himself, aspiring; Berrigan's hands coming out from his body like streams out of a mountain into valleys; four trout released and poured over the pool. Legget, trying to ease the descent of fish, caught them all, conscientiously, as if it were his test, allowing his entrance to the girl. All grasped, he dropped one, accidentally, as Berrigan watched the one fish fall slippery from Legget's fingers, his hand close, panicked, on air.

Berrigan watched it all, saw the fish plop into the thin dust coating the rock, saw Legget pick it up swiftly and clumsily, too quickly, as if he could still hide the fault. The raised fish left a thin imprint of fins, scales, gills in the dust, the shape of a thrown and landed body, the figure on rock of the trout, the place marked in the fall.

Then Berrigan departed, his netted fish distributing their colors on the mountain; he climbed up toward the white horns, where the snowline rose, and he slipped sideways into his valley toward his home.

BERRIGAN DESCENDED INTO THE VALLEY, like the mountain returning on itself, a reversal natural to the thaw's release. He saw his children playing among the long-bodied hounds. The dogs ran beside the creek, yapping, in a circle as Dutch and Dutchess dodged in and out, slipping through the line, through the figure the hounds described upon the grass. Far toward the western end of the valley, Berrigan could just make out three of the four horses and the mule grazing. He eased himself down rocky places, holding to stiff shrubs, picking his careful way. He could see Sawpootway below, under the small roof of her porch. She stitched a shirt, long sinews through the leather, the shirt Berrigan would wear later in his life. In the mid-afternoon, she worked her designs in the garment; the bone needles pierced leather with dyed white threads, as if she'd illustrate Berrigan in terms of claws, shaggy heads, her composed animals, apparently white bone, against the shirt, ponderous creatures moving through her life while, among repetitive white figures, brown vines wound like snakes to her pattern, so involved it seemed she wove her own long, pliant fingers into leather.

Berrigan heard a noise behind him and turned. Three hundred yards up the slope, a grizzly reared and stared toward the sewing woman. The figure of the bear moved in Berrigan like an old self he'd forgotten. Berrigan turned away, smiling to himself and unafraid. He thought of the woman's sewing. She'd woven cloth and plied her needles continuously, for twenty-one years, since they'd come to the valley in 1779. Before their crossing of the plains she'd had another man, a husband Berrigan had killed defending himself against that man and two others, had killed him with a half-breed's help: Sawpootway often said she'd eaten of that death, consumed her husband's life into her own: she said she hadn't aged a day since then. Berrigan knew she'd never eaten of that flesh, and also knew she seemed to age little since that day, or since the day her children were born. In the valley she'd entered an almost changeless life, after the pregnancy, as though that heaviness of children remained in her later thinness, in her singleness, amazing to Berrigan whose own life astonished him in alternations between breadth and thinness, flesh diminishing only to enlarge again—spring, summer, autumn, winter, spring—and he sometimes felt as if he, in occasional sickness and health among children and hounds, determined all the change she could know, her slight alterations, of the diminished pulse, while he aged a little more than she did, all her change only the growth of two children her body closed behind, and the alternations, rise and fall, of Berrigan himself; and all the repeated seasons had come to a kind of stillness in her, as if her heart had now little repulse, once flushed out in childbirth, opening—blood rushing up into her skin, surfacing—her heart, without a natural recourse to itself, like a flooded pool that wouldn't return to size, to its natural and limited shores.

Yet she'd become, and remained, thinner and whiter after her children were born; it was as though, after all, only her spirit remained thrown out, like tent flaps open to plains wind, her native wind, that wouldn't let flaps close.

Her stitching was patient and perfect and she worked it constantly, it seemed; she waited and dared an error to appear in the design, under fingers white as though her blood was white. She dared the false stitch to appear in her design, within the rhythm of her fingers, some false stitch she'd expected for years, an error to repulse the life she'd rushed into in that valley, as if she expected that error would make her single, without two children, without Berrigan or any man again, as she had once been, lying in a hut for her change from childhood, while her tribeswomen had watched; she'd expected a husband so eagerly, while the blood stained the buffalo grass beneath her knees.

Berrigan hadn't seen her extension when they'd entered the valley, coming from her tribe on the plains. But her body had already begun, without his notice, to swell with the children; then she labored in March when Berrigan worked, with the pulse of her labor, between her raised knees, and she'd had trouble expelling any child, her body reluctant to open. Her hands had lain, clenched, holding nothing, so fiercely, by themselves, like two hearts closed and bloodless beside her head, involuntary hearts compelling her blood; and she lost her will to the contractions, seizures of the womb and its opening, her pulse most dominant at the womb's dilation, mouth; for the center of her life had shifted, existing in the muscle of exit. Her child lived there.

The longest contraction had shown Berrigan the young head darkly, like the pupil of an eye, the small drenched figure emerging from his wife. When the shoulders appeared, themselves like childish closed fists, Berrigan handled them, pulling and lifting softly as the mother's will became one with the opening-out, with the muscle that released her child.

The light had diminished their candles, coming over mountains, an intruder Berrigan had forgotten to expect again, this day. The dawn seemed improvised, draining the birth of candlelight; and the child came into his open hands, noisy from the muscle. Sawpootway's body moved so bright in the dawn, when candles were diminished, in the bright body of the girl's birth.

The child had lived in his fingers, almost beyond the woman who wished only to close behind it, while Berrigan's steel blade, heated, cut quick as the life. Sawpootway called the child after me, for one man or boy they'd both known, altering my nickname to the child's gender, calling her Dutchess instead of Dutch, and believing once more, as she'd often believed—the child opening her in the long months—that she'd conceived my child purposefully, to fulfill an obsession; for in that old time on the plains, she believed she'd taken all her tribe's religion into herself, in that conception, that she was herself, after the act, all the aspiration of her people, that their dreams had stolen into her with the seed, as she'd stolen the seed from me. For a moment, in the birth, she regretted the sex of the child; for only a male could be the one she'd meant to be born from such an old act, to consummate her tribe and render the old religion obsolete beyond her, religion lost outside her body, the child become all that men must believe, through her. Then her obsession passed, and her daughter was before her, seen by the mother; yet, afterwards, an aura of that madness surrounded the girl child, the first born.

That dawn she'd believed Dutchess was to be the only child born; and she'd have closed her body over the birth, over a wound she'd caress deeply, holding her pain so closely it would mingle with the relief of afterbirth, and would become pleasure, at last only a gentle, diminished throb like her pulse; and her own life would resume.

Yet, after the girl, her body had continued whiter, like her doubled fists, as if all blood would be expelled in more opening out, and she'd learned painfully, through the slow, piercing rhythm, of the second child within her, one lingering for hours, more reluctant to leave womb and muscle. Dutchess had been laid down, near the mother, in soft fur. Berrigan, bewildered, watched, and learned, as the cleft flesh of the child's buttocks appeared in the woman, steadfast, stuck there like a remorse that wouldn't be expelled from her heart. The muscle held the boy. Only then had Berrigan believed he was there, the boy Sawpootway, in her pain, proclaimed after the girl. Berrigan was too absorbed in the child to be frightened, too intense in the woman's labor.

He had prepared so well for the event, the first birth and even, without foreknowledge, for this reluctance of birth, prepared in the aspiration of his flesh, making way in himself for offspring to come from the woman, from the opened mother, who lay gripped by her body before him, in an injured animal's pain of opening to the treatment of a man: on the broad bed he'd laid fresh skins, tanned only this early springtime; with carved wooden tongs he'd dropped revolving stones, steaming through water, into large pottery bowls Sawpootway wove on the wheel. Even with the stones his hands were tender, even as they were with fish, flesh, human children and woman; and it was difficult for him to determine how he distinguished between things, between stones and children, with what subtleties of touch; he put fingers upon the buttocks, wondering at the child who was so doubled over, and he touched the female skin surrounding the child. What difference did his fingers tell between the child's flesh and the woman's? Berrigan couldn't answer; yet knew, in the pulse beneath the tips of his fingers, the difference in the sameness of flesh. There was little more he could do but touch tenderly, watching the closed eyelids and fists of the woman. He had already reheated more water. He waited, kneeling between her knees, as she labored, while the boy child gradually emerged, such a long advent. And Sawpootway had named him before the muscle released him, when Berrigan touched small buttocks, penis, testicles, and told what the sex was.

Dutch, at last, came loose, urged by Berrigan's fingers and by the muscle in the woman, came already named into Berrigan's hands, but unbreathing, his toes stuck up toward the eyes. In fear, Berrigan saw Sawpootway, her strained body suspended in the last contraction, as if she'd expelled her body in the child and could not retrieve it. Her body, like her fists, stayed in that taut extension, that last clench of her opening: she was lost into that child, whiter than he was; he was torn from her. Her fists, opening after, had been closed, as her body was not closed now, and she'd still have liked, more than ever, to close her flesh over the hard birth. Her blood soaked the fur and the deerskins, it stained the bed; pain faded inward, and pain's connection with her body and child forgotten.

Berrigan was afraid for his child, and the expression of the woman worried him. The world had become silent, the first child sleeping, the mother too still, and he thought his son dead, though he didn't believe in that death. There was a blue film over the boy's eyes, Berrigan imagined. He straightened the small legs; he licked the eyes, ears, mouth and would have taken the boy's head, whole, in his mouth. He blew into the nostrils, cracked the buttocks with his palms, caressed the thin chest, stroked the small genitals and, at last, inserted his smallest finger between the buttocks; and the child gasped. So air, sucked in, had flowed out again after the shock of Berrigan's finger, establishing the double rhythm of Dutch's living breath, like the pulse of his mother in labor or the rhythm of his father's blood in fear.

Then Berrigan had placed both children by Sawpootway. They slept near her neck like obverse emblems of her wakefulness; for she couldn't sleep until the next dawn, though she lay with eyes closed throughout the hours of light and darkness; then she tried to convince the twins to take her milk. On the third day she succeeded and they sucked.

But the children had slept soon, fresh from the womb, and Sawpootway's awake, purged body lay blue-white, almost transparent, like the young boy's skin, like china dishes, as Berrigan cleaned up the blood. He wrapped them all in clean fur and, weary, moved through the steam of hot water he'd overprepared, as if he'd expected a third child. For a time Berrigan hadn't been sure a third wouldn't come. All the bleeding had stopped at last, with the end of that small trickle where the boy had torn her. She had little to say in the long hours before she slept.

Berrigan sighed and watched the sleeping children, Dutch and Dutchess alive, and watched Sawpootway, who hadn't died either. Now she slept the birth, between her children. Berrigan held his hands before him, at diminished candle stubs and snuffed the lights as the dawn dimmed them again. The candles had gone squat in wax they descended into, as if they'd enter their own sleep after children were born. He held his fingers at the base of candles, imprinting them on wax, as if he'd seal the event, then removed his hands to study impressions he made in yellow tallow. From her sleep, Sawpootway called his name, raising her torso, and he saw her head's imprint on the fur. She fell back, into deeper sleep. Berrigan, too tense to sleep after his long labor and watch, saw his family sleeping, and moved, that morning, through a mist or dream of himself as father, in a new air, feeling out this turn of his life. His family, though, seemed far removed from him in afterbirth, like inhuman things, creatures almost without relation to him. He couldn't really see what difference they made; yet felt some change he couldn't have described except as a change in the air. He was not sure he liked this new medium, of fatherhood, he moved in, breathing the birth of his children who lay with their mother in furs. At noon, he was suddenly sleepy, unable to keep his eyelids up; so he piled skins in a corner for his own rest; and he dreamed only of the hours he'd passed. In those dreams, his body felt torn from him.

More than twenty years later, Orcus Berrigan descended into the valley, appearing, as his children raised their heads and saw him. He waved and the hounds approached him. By the creek, under a lone cottonwood, the children waited in a gap of the firs, as Sawpootway opened her own eyes, her vision emerging; she looked up at the man, yet continued her work. She didn't need her eyes for sewing nor hands yet for Berrigan's approach. The blue hounds—three, then the fourth, Cinco—lifted their forelegs to his shoulders and chest. They licked his face until Berrigan ducked beneath their bodies, striding through the hounds toward his children. As if in a vision, he saw:

Sawpootway, eternally sewing, sits beside her daughter, beside Dutchess in labor. The young girl's eyes enlarge, her forehead shines, as Sawpootway at last puts down her work, though her fingers still stitch through air before she places her hands upon her daughter's moving womb. Together their bodies assume a rhythm to expel the child. A baby appears, dark as his mother's hair, and so like her, as if Dutchess, transformed, becomes a male child. Legget enters the cabin and, without looking at the unnamed child, asks where Berrigan and Dutch are. Sawpootway sways from one foot to another, the child asleep in her arms; she sings a lullaby of her tribe, the soft voice weaving patterns of sound in air, as her body sways more and more into the tune. Her arms are even darker than the child she holds, limbs transfused with her risen blood. Dutchess hears Legget's voice. She raises herself to elbows, and angrily calls her brother's name. Legget wipes the sweat from his eyes as he'd remove a spider web fallen on his vision, and glancing at the child as if he's embarrassed, he leaves by the door, backing out, palms thrust forward toward Dutchess, as if to ward her from him. He averts his head, turning to see the snow descending from the high mountain horns, and he throws his arms up toward the mountain, fists as tiny as a boy's, his arms flailed in wide arcs about his body as if he signaled the mountain peaks themselves, or someone hidden between them, veiled by the snow; then he covers his red face with fingers and palms. Whirling about blindly, he returns to the cabin, plunging to the door. He removes his hands to see, shouting for Dutchess; but the new mother and the grandmother have closed over the child in protection and gone from his life. Panicked, he runs back out, enters the snow which covers him like a sheet he himself might have pulled down upon him.

Berrigan, walking toward the creek, looked toward the cabin in confusion. He'd seen, since I imagine: the birth of his grandchild; the flight of the women with child; Legget's snow burial. It had all slid over his mind, like the water of the pooled river around his thighs, like water he might wash with and let dry, arriving home in the heat of that afternoon; the scene evaporated as swiftly as it had come. Sawpootway was still there, sewing, and he continued toward the place by the creek where his children, Dutch and Dutchess, waited beneath one cottonwood tree; he saw the roots rise at their feet, buds beginning to appear on the limbs above them, soon to veil the tree in leaves. Now that he was close enough he could see a few small twigs spin down past their heads, and he looked at the treetop. Behind the cabin, chickens pecked in the yard, the single rooster like a watchman over scabby, darting necks of hens. He held up the fish he'd caught, in the net, and his children—Dutchess spreading her smile wide like the fish net; Dutch, taking in sharp breath inaudible in the distance—moved toward him slowly, hesitating as if, shyly, they didn't quite believe the fish in the net, the trout so multiple and colored by the sun behind their heads, as if they feared the fish might dissolve if they approached their father too quickly, as if their fingers, wishing only to touch, might slip through their father's catch.

Under descended snow, Legget sleeps near the cabin, and he dreams of them all: Sawpootway sewing designed leather, Berrigan with fish extended, the children more confident now and running, those hounds blue and obedient at Berrigan's heels. Legget remembers the scene he never saw, the scene they lived. The blue-white snow, unmarked now by tracks, in the dark night lies smooth upon him, and he recalls how he entered the cabin where the child was born, when Berrigan and Dutch were gone.

Berrigan shook his head; he'd seen and forgotten, like water he washed in once, Legget comforted in snow; and now felt his children take the ends of his gathered net in their fingers, holding the trout between them, admiring his catch of bright fish. Sawpootway leaned toward them when they turned, her feet shifting at the base of the chair, her body inclined, through the shadow of the porch post, her body through sunlight moted in the rapid, foot-raised dust. The rooster, hounds, Berrigan, and the children had approached and arrived at the porch, by the sewing woman. Berrigan turned his catch in the sun, and she approved with her eyes and with the stillness of fingers in her lap.

IN HER OWN TONGUE, SAWPOOTWAY said she knew Nat Legget. Berrigan had pulled another chair out to the porch and sat beside her, while Dutch and Dutchess cleaned fish at the creek. Sawpootway said Legget reminded her of a red-bottomed monkey and, with no sense of contradiction, said he fathers forth snakes who have no mothers. Mothers have disappeared, hidden in the earth again. Serpents crawl forth out of the dead bosoms, like worms from the decay of women; Legget peers down for them in holes both damp and cold. He has no power in winter when the earth, like his future life, freezes over. His is the power of warmest seasons only, beginning in this thaw, this season like the melting of a woman's bones and flesh, the season coming to the flood Legget loves, and shall drown in.

Unpuzzled—since he'd heard its substance all before, last year for the first time and every time after when he'd mention Legget, seldom mentioned now— Berrigan asked how Legget could conceive such children, as if he were both father and mother. Berrigan was not interested in his question, only asked it, foolishly, so she'd continue; he indulged her much. So, Sawpootway continued, urged on to say that Legget eats a woman's half-roasted heart, and conceives himself. A wolf, gray, with bent ears, emerges like his child, doughy among the serpents, getting shape slowly.

Berrigan said he saw there were serpents and a wolf. He mulled the animals over, as if she'd surprised him. Sawpootway repeated, serpents and wolf. The father of them backs through his own heart, retreats through his own body and sinks out at last through himself, as though flesh collapsed, dissolved, and left only the thin bones on a surface of water.

Berrigan spoke of the animals only in English: children like snakes and a wolf, no living mothers. He had listened carefully to the woman's talk, to her thought. He'd frowned, listening to notions of Legget, pretending he'd never heard them. He'd shrugged, wondering again what to make of her words. Again he told her Legget had come. He told her Legget had come again.

Sawpootway said she was afraid of Legget, even of Berrigan's speech of the trapper. She covered her ears with her palms, so the sound of Berrigan's speech couldn't enter with ease, while he asked what they would do about his coming. She looked down, frustrated, at the sewing in her lap; she couldn't touch it without removing her hands and listening to Berrigan. Then she would listen. She took up a thin thong of leather and a needle of bone. She spoke and Berrigan, who'd been telling her to take her hands from her ears, became silent again. She said that the trapper had once had a daughter of his own, born of the water. Berrigan let all her contradictions go over him like that water and picked out, as best he could, the intention of her speech. She said Legget had thrown his daughter in an oven where she'd bled ever since, from her womb. And no one will touch her. The trapper had departed, betraying her, as if he'd died long before she was born. This had been his past and it is his only future, repeating his departure and the girl's confinement, no new life to change his luck, no lover ever arriving to release her. The cold is always before him like a promise of rest; she burns in her own body forever unconsumed: unproductive, untransformed, serpents brood while a wolf's rough tongue runs over his fangs.

Suddenly Sawpootway changed the talk, as if she repented of her wild words, and they spoke of the sewing she did. So inconsequential words spread between them, like a garment barely disguising a quarrel, the woman speaking in her native tongue and

Berrigan in his, as if a fabric they wove like Berrigan's new shirt was the only significant thing in their relation, and even that fabric insubstantial. They saw the twins returning from the creek, coming with cleaned trout in a basket swung between them. The chickens feasted, near the water, on remains of fish, on intestines. Shadows of western peaks, as if laid down to their rest, stretched out toward the eastern mountain, overlaying the faraway horses and mule, and Berrigan thought the twin-peaked mountain's shadow must fall now well over Legget, like a sign of Sawpootway's reluctance and her fear of him. He told her that the trapper wished to speak with her, to explain himself, to persuade her. He'd waited for just this moment to say that, and to say, hoping to convince her this time, that she'd never even seen the trapper. Berrigan, taking up, for the moment, Legget's cause, remained confused about his own wish in the matter; he half-believed Sawpootway's images of the trapper.

Sawpootway said she'd seen Legget every nighttime for years past, had known him, long ago, in her own life. So had Berrigan, she said, squinting at him, as if she thought he deceived her, as if she wondered what motive he could have, pretending he hadn't known Legget long before the previous summer.

Berrigan denied it. He said she thought of someone else, who Legget wasn't, no more than Berrigan was, or she was. He said Legget could not be who she thought, must be someone other.

The children brought their basket of cleaned fish. Dutch held them out to his father. He said to look at them. Sawpootway hadn't answered him, so Berrigan turned from her, and tentatively inserted two fingers into the slit body of a trout. The trout colors dimmed as night came on, as if their light returned into the small, cut bodies, as if the flesh of trout were pools they turned their lives about in, revolving to swim away through themselves, into the death of fish, where Berrigan's fingers couldn't follow.

Dutchess had left them, going out toward the chicken shed, she said to feed chickens Berrigan knew had already fed on insides of fish, and he wondered why she departed, so softly; he seemed to forget how she'd looked—either in arrival, or standing beside her brother, or when she'd left them—as though he'd never known her features. He wondered if she'd heard them speak of her and of someone named Legget who was interested in her. Berrigan imagined a long curving line through the late afternoon sky, a path like the flight of the fish or the smiles of his children, or like that of the star that appeared in the west. He looked at his son, who still held the basket for probing, the young man's body so erect, hard and piercing, as if he could walk through the cottonwood tree—or through the pines, their trunks like a mist, a shower of green needles, those spines dividing upon him, like water reluctant to injure his body. Berrigan removed his fingers from the fish and took the basket from his son. He gave Sawpootway the slit trout, and followed her, as they rose, to the door of their house. She entered while he lingered in the doorway.

Berrigan saw their son still watched, as if he could see his mother inside. Then Dutch turned from the porch, and Berrigan watched his back retreat around the corner. He shouted after the young man, about to say to milk the goats, but he didn't say it and Dutch, after glancing back, continued. Dutch laughed, going toward his sister and the chickens for a purpose unknown to his father.

Berrigan entered the house, where the woman set

the fish down, where she covered the dead trout bodies with a patterned cloth. Berrigan took the net and hung it from beams on the wall. Sawpootway sat on the bed Berrigan had made of the pine wood. She folded her hands and spoke to herself, inaudibly, as if she mumbled prayers like Berrigan's English mother. She was the same when he left her, not yet cooking the fish, when he lifted his ax from the wall pegs and walked out to the woodpile on the eastern side. He could hear the chickens cackling behind the house and thought he also heard, beyond the chickens, his children shout, playing again with the long-snouted, blue-white dogs.

Soon, after the first sounds of the ax, the slow rhythm, Berrigan's son joined him. The two men split the wood, taking turns, the grain breaking upon itself, beneath their strokes, under the blue lift and fall of sharp metal. The long-handled ax flashed, as one man watched the other work. Gradually, in the darkness, Berrigan's turn became so short, no one swung the ax but Dutch; and there would be wood for days.

BERRIGAN, IN BED, ROLLED ONTO HIS stomach, his breath coming harsh into his pillow, his ears half submerged in the down of chicken feathers beneath the cloth cover; and Sawpootway talked. The night, by the window, was so soft, moist, so dark and warm, as though the house lay hard-edged like a coin concealed in someone's palm. Sawpootway's voice wove through the silence of night, coming to Berrigan's ears as if through water, like a fish winding its way carefully through a fish-known course; and it had become almost too difficult for Berrigan, where he lay, to endure, after so many hours of talk, the Indian tongue that was foreign, difficult for him to complete the transformation, to keep the attention required to understand her words, much less her intention difficult in her words. The pillow muffled his sighs, as he lost the thread in various instants.

He knew she'd already said, repeatedly, that she remembered. She said Legget had arrived when her tribe's hope, and hers, for a husband, had been abandoned. No man would touch her; because her father was the poisoner, too deadly to be worth the power obtained through her. The women of the tribe had already tried to console her for the loss of all men, when Legget, she said, had entered swiftly, like a ferret nosing out long-eared rabbits, strong-haunched jacks of the plains, trading with the Indians for hides to complete his lazy season's meager haul. He brought metallic things in the barter for skins. There were no mountains anywhere in sight, only the sun and wind above forever receding plainsland, and the brightness of Legget's small metal suns filled that landscape and her with ambition and desire.

She said that after the trapper got drunk with her father, Snakesnorter, who vomited toward sunrise, she awoke and was almost gone from her people, bought with small shininess, bright things worked upon by hands as if man made tiny gods for himself. So she escaped, and never tasted the poison her father mixed for her; and her father didn't taste her poisoned body. She watched that old man bite into metal pieces strung together on a cord, until he was satisfied, until he died years later, just before she returned. She found him rendered in pieces she mourned and will always recompose in dreams, as she'd tried to remake him with parts of the war chief, her father's murderer, whom she'd killed in revenge, to make her father's body whole again.

Berrigan had already recognized that vision of Legget and her old life, of memory confused, and entered, as before, into what he'd heard so often.

Once more he pretended he was that husband, before all others, the one she'd waited for in the maiden lodge, one come before the trapper, LeGuey, anticipating his bargain, come before the husband she mistook Legget for. Filling out her tale, imagining a past, he urges his body toward a solitary lodge, specially prepared for this time of her life. Sawpootway is waiting for a husband, and he comes to her as she lingers by the food door, which opens to Berrigan's fingers. His hands are like fish picking through tight rocky places, their difficult route to the girl who's waiting. His hands appear to her in the high door, in the small door far from the earth, fingers feeling for her in the darkness of the lodge, where she bleeds. She stands upon tiptoe and swiftly puts his fingers, as many as possible, into her mouth. Berrigan, who can't see her, is frightened, and he attempts to withdraw the dampened hand, but Sawpootway, biting hard to hold him, sucks the fingers she controls. Long before her husband, LeGuey, or Legget, arrives, they escape together into the mountains, into the valley where she bears him two children, twin boy and girl named Dutch and Dutchess. Within Berrigan's pretense of being her first husband, his children's faces remain obscure to him, like something only the future knows.

Then Berrigan, unsleeping, undreaming, realized Sawpootway had become silent, after he'd entered the vison, a silence like hands cupped over his ears. Involuntarily, afraid he'd failed to answer an important question, he spoke her name, Sawpootway. In answer, she crawled upon him, stretched her body out, as though she tried to match his length and width with her own, spreading herself to measure the man. Berrigan murmured that he was sorry if he hadn't heard her, that he must have dozed away a moment while she talked. What had she said? He asked her.

Her body relaxed, returning to its own dimensions. Her lips moved near his ear, saying she'd said she would propose a test for Legget.

Berrigan asked what it was, not really caring, now that her body was with his body, now that he probed, without caution, within her: for she'd turned to receive him.

Now she spoke again, this time of testing, never disclosing an exact meaning beyond some few questions she'd ask Legget; and Berrigan turned his body, weaving beneath her. He watched her torso rising, till her head, in dark hair and night, was lost to him, so her voice spoke to him from the distant sky, where stars were clear through the window and piercing, though they gave no light to the bed, and her breasts slapped alongside his face, long, heavy creatures of that darkness. He'd entered her into a former time of their life together, into a previous vision of a pale rose opening in a black sky. He wondered at the image of old experience, of the days they were first together, in the woods by the Mississippi, and going up the Missouri. He couldn't see her face; she was one with the sky. Her shape blotted stars.

Later, they lay silently and heard Dutch and Dutchess talking from their beds, behind the taut skin wall that had stood for years between parents and children. Then they slept, and Berrigan's fingers curled gradually to make fists like pine knots upon Sawpootway's belly. He dreamed something he wouldn't remember, something in which unintelligible old voices murmur to him, like animals laughing behind the scene, or giddy women whispering love like a poison in his ears, voices too inaudible, soft-tongued, to wake him from the dream they make.

Berrigan's son's body, blue and white lightning, pierces the length of a tree, a voice screaming close to another's ear. For an instant that light stands out and becomes still, like ice in a crevice, blue like the hounds that have always been family companions, white like the hounds; the tree divides and falls without a sound, not even the sound of thunder, as if the noise of the light were too loud for humans to hear, without even the sound of voices hiding in Berrigan's soft and furry ear, not even those female voices that whisper so softly in dreams of forbidden love.

Behind the house the single rooster crowed, and Berrigan woke, thinking dawn had already come over the mountain's twin peaks, through the pale reddened horns. He rose, discovered the false dawn; yet went and sat on the porch to clean his gun. The woman, he knew, would go with him this morning to meet Legget. He didn't know what it was she planned: at least she would go. He was still sleepy. She would tell Dutch soon what was meant to happen, but Berrigan was still too sleepy to wonder what she'd tell his son, or to worry about it. She'd said she must tell Dutch, and Berrigan said she could do as she wanted, just so they went together to see Legget. When she saw him she would know he wasn't who she thought. She had never been married to him, a silly belief of hers, arguing madness that had persisted through years, kept down by the surface of their life in the valley, kept down by will.

Vague images of old danger, unidentifiable, became

present in Berrigan, clearer and clearer until he saw again how three men once attacked him, her husband, bewilderingly, one of them, with Berrigan's former fellow-troopers, Smith and Thompson; how, with the half-breed's sudden help, he'd killed them, folding their bodies back, with the strength of his spine and arms; how he'd seemed to tread upon them; how Drake, or Pawkittew, the half-breed, had pecked at their faces; Drake's flint knife articulated strange signs. Somehow, Berrigan had survived that time, that fight which came upon him like a punishment, after his first time with Sawpootway.

When the dawn's true light came, coloring the mountain peaks like trout sides, Berrigan laid down his rags, his rod, the gun, blew the candle out he'd worked by, and rose, between cockcrows, and because he wanted something to do, went to feed chickens entering the yard, and to milk the goats. In passing, he heard Sawpootway already waking Dutch to explain her design. Later, Berrigan would think, as her plan was effected, that he had no choice but to go along and, anyway, what harm could come of her small joke, of her woman's trick on Legget? She was so often melancholy, he realized, that a joke, a simple ruse, seemed good in her, indicating an improvement of mind, as though old obsessions Berrigan glimpsed in her, through her talk of Legget, fell like water, away from her body, her unreasonable fear of Legget, and of the past, failing through jest, to leave her healthy, as though, in an afterlife, she came reborn and guiltless. She'd often carried Berrigan's body into sleep, deep after their sex. Reborn, she'd led a way to new life.

BEFORE NOON, THE AIR WAS STILL COLD. Berrigan stood, ready to speak, with one hand on the tree bark. He leaned on his gun, peering at Legget across the water, or looking down at the woman who'd huddled at his feet, her arms squeezing her knees, back against the tree, and her eyes invisible until she bent back her head and spoke, to the clouds overhead or the ascending sun. Berrigan, looking into her face, translated her question to Legget: where did he come from, and who were his people?

For a moment, Legget only appeared to be aware of his mule searching for vegetation up a slope and harming thick lips with the stiff, fallen needles. Then Legget asked if that was all they wanted to know. He saw Berrigan look to Sawpootway for her answer, and he wondered why, though she obviously understood the English language, she wouldn't speak it. Couldn't she speak it well enough to want to? Was she ashamed of her awkwardness in that tongue? Now she didn't answer, only waited for his reply. So Legget said his father was a farmer from New York State, his mother dead years past, gone swiftly from his youth as though, once he'd been given out, she no longer belonged in the world her child came to. He was born in New York colony before the Revolution. He had fought with some distinction, a Colonial trooper. He had nothing in his past to hide, not even that hate for the woman his father married when old. What more natural hate could a boy have than that? What reason could he have to hide that hate? Almost a year ago he'd come to this country for fur, then seen the girl from far away. He could not forget her, but Sawpootway had forbidden him. Why should her parents scorn him, without a chance? Let him speak to her, now that he had returned as promised.

Berrigan waited for more questions. In one hand Sawpootway squeezed a brown pine cone. She studied the trapper who squatted across the pool. She studied the mule that, rejoining the trapper, gazed at her and Berrigan. All their eyes were on her. Noon was arriving as it had the day before, but now no fish cut the chill air, no net rose heavy with trout from the water; yet the pool still swirled and rushed on, and the sun occasionally cut through clouds to strike the pool in reflection. Just before this noon, words seemed physical to Sawpootway, like bodies with weight, heavy steam suspended in brief sunlight—words out of silence, the silvery, apparent breath shaped by her lungs, like passing clouds that shadowed the mountains or like fish Berrigan brought home, words issued from her mouth; for she spoke again, first in the order of speech, her white puff reshaped by Berrigan for Legget's ears, while she studied the formation, in air, of her speech and her translator's. She wanted to know if Legget had ever had a woman. And she watched for the puff of his breath to form, out of the pursed, considering mouth.

Yes, he'd loved one who died, as all he loved died, like his mother out of his life. Yes, a girl had once been promised to him by his father's friend and by her own mouth, but she'd died before the possibility of marriage. Legget had only touched her forehead briefly with his fingers, brushing damp hair back, and his lips had grazed her cheekbone when no one, not even she, watched him. She lay near death in that moment, then fell far from him, never waking; so he could never tell her how he'd touched her. And

Legget closed his lips, having told more than he'd meant to tell.

Hadn't she been an Indian girl? Berrigan translated the question with no comment. Sawpootway screwed her eyes up to peer over the water.

Legget said she'd been as white as he was, as the clouds.

Who was her father?

A doctor of horses, cows, chickens, animals of those valley farms.

Sawpootway said something else. She smiled. When Legget asked, Berrigan said she'd said yes.

Then they would let him meet Dutchess? The clouds piled before the sun, white puffs of cumulus merging, bulking like the mountain above or like Berrigan over the woman, the sun hiding like Sawpootway's huddled plan.

In Legget's imagination, a vague, dark figure emerges slowly above the peaks and turns white like the ice. Legget guessed the figure is Dutchess. Last summer he'd told them he'd return in spring to know her. So they would let him meet her now, he told himself. That was all he asked.

Berrigan said yes, though he frowned and shook his head as though to clear his ears of water.

Legget said he knew the best place to cross upstream. He would come over to them, and to her. Together they'd go to the valley. He'd prove himself welcome; they wouldn't be sorry to have him.

Berrigan, interpreting what Sawpootway said, still frowned, hesitated, then said to wait, they'd bring someone to him. He translated what the woman said: it would be like a surprise. She laughed, her long hair thrust between her knees, a solid body, a dark column

36

flowing downward. Berrigan squeezed the bark of the tree, felt its print in his palm.

Legget thought Berrigan wanted to say something of his own. Legget said he would wait, if someone came today.

Sawpootway spoke: Berrigan said yes, it would be today; it would be now.

Would someone be alone, without parents?

Berrigan nodded, and bent to the woman, to softly say he didn't like it, the trick they'd play on an innocent man.

She said that Legget wasn't innocent.

Berrigan said Legget was not who she thought. Couldn't she see that, now she'd questioned him? He believed she must see it.

Sawpootway whispered, almost hissing, that Legget lied to them. She sat among the black, wet roots, threw back her dark hair, and whispered he lied, in every breath like smoke.

Berrigan turned away in anger. She rose. Sawpootway followed him from the pool. Silent, he went up the river, occasionally glancing back at the trapper, who was now only waiting, eager to wait. She pleaded with Berrigan to return; she wanted him with her. It was only a joke, she said. But he'd turned against her, deaf to her argument.

Legget followed their departure with his eyes, unable to hear them. He wondered, only for a moment, what they spoke. Then he glanced up the mountain where a figure clears against the snow, between the horns, and Legget sighed at that image, like a release to him, his flow and his rhythm freed in a personal thaw, his opening to the figure. A young woman slowly clambers down, just as he'd imagined her. She arrives too swiftly to be quite natural, and touches his lips with her tongue. She licks his eyes as if she'd clear eyes of all old illusion, healing the membrane. In silence, her breath forms like speech above their shoulders. Legget rubbed his brow as if that were her body under the thin, white clothes, caresses slower than her mountain descent.

Clouds covered the two peaks of the mountain; they blended in sunlight to make one white body, while Berrigan and the woman, Sawpootway, in shadow, disappeared up the gorge. A cloud descends on Legget like a woman's body or the breath of Sawpootway's lying speech.

Out of sight, Sawpootway laughed harshly into the palm of her hand; Berrigan rubbed his hand on his pants leg. Light hair grows between Sawpootway's rubbing fingers; and she imagined it hangs down from her chin, silky hair of deceit, and she felt like her son descending to Legget.

A figure did appear upriver, in white veil and dress, a bride ridiculous in the rough gorge, on Legget's side of the river, a preposterous image, separated from dream, skins and fur showing faintly through edges of the white clothing; for Dutch had hidden nearby in the gorge. Dutch, in the disguise of his mother's dress and veil, could only have fooled Legget's already clouded eyes, when Legget imagined his desire imprinted on Dutch's unseen features.

SHE SAYS SHE DOES WANT TO, SHE'S hungry, walking so far from the valley. She bends toward him. Behind the veil, her eyes reveal, in light,

what Legget dreamed. Her mouth is long with his desire. Legget said he'd caught, especially for her, four
fish like those her father gave him. Legget had split
their bellies and cleaned them, before she'd come;
now he pierced them with two sticks. At noon, above
the pool, Legget and Dutch held the food before
them, over fire. Legget smiled and believed Dutchess
smiles in return. There were no shadows and the tree,
across the water, screamed with birds among its green
needles, four mountain jays plucking the needles.

They ate, as Legget stared at the veil lifted to the
lowered mouth, when Dutch ate, apparently shy.
Above the pool, the sun cleared, and their breath, between bites, was invisible. Fish vanished into their
mouths, and they let the bones fall beside them.
Legget was afraid she would choke on one, some
small bone through the long mouth he'd glimpsed beneath the veil, bone falling to pierce the loved throat;
he had no bread for her to swallow. Legget asked
what kind of birds those were that looked so black at
noon, needles like twigs in their beaks. In that tree,
he'd imagined, the rooster towered, indicating the girl
and boy, felling needles. Real needles lay under the
tree across the water, no longer green but as brown as
the hard pine fruit carpeting the rock. Legget remembered that he or someone else had imagined that scene
of girl, boy, and rooster up the lodge-pole pine. He remembered how Berrigan had hoisted the fish in the
net. The father had gone away now and the mother.
He thought they must have hidden somewhere,
watching like the jays, as the white horns watched
him.

Berrigan's son watched Legget, and smiled behind
his veil. He asked if Legget knew who he was.

Legget said yes, he knew, and she would be happy

with him, if she would. He'd come to marry. Will she have him?

Dutch didn't know what to say. Even more embarrassed, he said yes, as if accidentally, then laughed as though, in that affirmation, he'd found a malicious pleasure he'd never known before.

Legget's fingers moved toward Dutch's mouth, sliding under the cloth. He felt where the tongue lay, as still as a sleeping child. Dutch spat those fingers out. Legget took his hand away, ashamed.

Dutch asked again if Legget recognized him.

Yes, and he, Legget, tore the veil, and the rifle barrel, seized, fell on Dutch's head. Legget gripped the neck of the boy; it swelled, like a serpent, on the ground. Once Legget had imagined green needles fall on Dutch's body, like a fine spray of water, a shower of a woman's hair.

Sawpootway will ask if anything will harm Dutch, and all things will say no, except the green needles: Dutch died to Legget's fingers as he saw, on the rocky ground, the spines of fish and a single, sharp jay's feather. He surrendered to the prickling in his throat, while Legget squeezed. Dutchess embraces Legget, who's grown hard like her brother's body was before he fell to the gun barrel and the fingers. Dutch could see that. Fallen to the rifle barrel, he melted like the mountain in thaw, or was pounded by Legget's fingers down the earth. He lay on the rock and the sun enters the pool like a dog, licking its paws, as though they're wounded. The dogs bark in the valley, among cockcrow and the cackle of hens, the baa of goats and whinny of the horses, the mule's whine. The girl, in the cabin alone, sews what her mother once did. Berrigan and Sawpootway had disappeared.

Legget stood up, lifting his gun only to drop it;

and the mule shied to the sound of metal on rock. The unconscious boy breathed too softly, as the mule approached to nuzzle the now visible features with heavy, dark lips, as if the mouth of the boy were grass on the mountain, found at last, some vegetation for an animal. The jays flew with needles in their beaks, as Legget ran to the water, gathered it in cupped hands. Water leaked out through his fingers, then he could only smear damp palms and fingers on the bared head and face.

For a time Legget stood and listened to the jays, to the mule's slow hooves, and to the river; then he bent to the boy with purpose, ashamed and angry to have been so deceived. He bound Dutch hand and foot with ropes to the mule, tied before the pack. He'd had more than enough, he told himself. No girl was worth such difficulty or sorrow, such deception. Only revenge was, sweet as the revenge on his father's wife, meticulous revenge, subtle as women.

The mountain left behind, the mule bore Dutch, as Legget led, apparently no burden now on his progress, the boy in departure soft and light, as if Dutch's weight remained behind with the mountain, in the place he'd fallen. So they passed down, beyond the bend, deserting sun, pool, pine tree, invisible words and half-eaten fish, the loud birds and the images Legget had once seen among the branches.

But the girl in the veil, once imagined, still holds her lunch on a stick. Legget still sits there, fingers lingering in her mouth, and he feels her rounded tongue and the rough edges of her blue-white teeth in the wide mouth. The river pools and creeps like a beaten mule or hound. The five jays sing the mountain's thaw, while the boy was bound to Legget's mule, among other trappings.

Berrigan and Sawpootway, who'd disappeared, as if into another time, returned to find nothing, no image of their son under new clouds, except signs of the brief struggle, of the boy surprised by Legget, of his new softness on the rocks: those fish, half-eaten, scattered among their bones to lie in thin dust, the fish Berrigan lifted to reveal their marks on the rock, as though he read omens. Sawpootway wailed, so high she was almost silent, and she spread her body down. With arms and legs, she stroked the pattern, like a bird's or angels, the method of her grief obliterating signs with the mark of her own body. Then she seemed to sleep, suddenly, as Berrigan watched. Soon he woke her, if she slept, with water borne from the river in his hat. She raised her head. Before she could speak, he said he would go after Dutch and return him. Berrigan, turning without her answer, made for the bend.

The shadow of the mountain fell toward her and toward the broken fish, and Sawpootway lay a long time where she was. Then, slowly, as if her feet were hurt, already lost, she too pursued, as night obscured their trail. It was no time to be sure of her acts. She didn't think of Dutchess alone in the valley.

DUTCHESS HELD THE FAT, SPECKLED egg, matted with straw and yoke; her fingers curled, taking its round, the pressure of the small end hard and comforting to her palm. She wasn't worried; she'd often been alone with hounds and chickens, with chores. She peered from under the shelter. In the west, mountains shadowed that end of the valley, the sun almost down behind them; she couldn't see the animals, horses, and mule, of the upper pasture any more. She'd expected people home long before, and now, having dawdled, she hurried with the eggs, plucking them from nests like fruit, fallen, she had to snatch up swiftly, before it rotted. More than once she'd plunged her quick hand into the warmth beneath a setting hen, the animal clucking in reluctance, the animal head wary like a snake's, even the beak like a third suspicious eye. She thrust the eggs into the darkness of her straw basket. As the hounds watched, from the door, Dutchess finished her gathering. She ran all the way to the house, the rooster and hounds at her heels—long-bodied hounds easily loping, the cock in ragged bounds.

She left her basket, and took the lantern and pail toward a western rise of ground, to a small, side gully of the creek, where the she-goats waited to be milked. When she knelt with her bucket, the hounds squatted down on their haunches; the rooster, the unnamed creature, scratched up the dust, grass blades spewed around. It was nearly dark there.

Two pregnant nannies cropped grass in the gully, hobbled within reach of the water, two gray goats near their time giving little milk now. The billy had died early in winter, and the family had eaten his meat even that morning. Dutchess knelt to them. White fluid steamed into the wood.

Above her, a light, flung out of the eastern darkness, an angel or bird plummeting down to the mountain, spread like a body on the saddle-peaks, and was gone, departed, a star shot out. The darkness weighed on her arms. So she labored on at her milking, unaware that the vision of that strange light had entered her body. With a twinge under her heart that she wouldn't free her hands to stroke, she studied, for distraction, the near, lantern-lit figures of the red cock and the blue and white hounds. In the circle of light, she imagined something grown, in her body, from the previous vision of falling light.

Fruit falls onto the ground, long drops squirted from a pear tree, like swollen white needles. Then fruit is rounded again. Dutchess, with a long mouth, comes much later, alone, and she bites into the rotten part, her white teeth into that softness, breaks the pale skin where the large end rested on damp earth.

Dutchess smiled at the image that had come, un-willed as if it had volition of its own. She finished the first nanny, shaking out the last, difficult drops. She removed her unfilled bucket, then stood, gazing at the high, pink saddle in the last sunlight.

Dutchess, deserted, knelt to the second goat, the elder one, and played this new milk into the old of the bucket, teats pressed by her fingers, pulled by hands, as Cinco and Hasty scuffled in the grass, dust, and shrubs, as the cock pecked at earth between his toes. The second goat, like the first, niggardly with milk, in the late pregnancy, stood patiently, as if she lingered forever at the lip of her birth, undisturbed by the world beyond.

After milking, Dutchess looked about in darkness, and wondered why no one came home. She walked to-ward the house in darkness that seemed as heavy around her light as water would; she wound, slowly, through rocks near the creek, among pines. The stars struck down hard, bright material bodies of light, inhuman beams to pierce the valley like needles; she felt she could pluck down the streaks like long irises bending to her, quick stars as though angels shot long-fingered wrists out of sleeves, like milk spurting and suddenly frozen, thrust into the valley to break on her fingers or eyes.

Her long fingers curled to the handle, tighter, and Dutchess carried the bucket into the house. The moon hadn't risen when the rooster returned to his yard, where the hens, their beaks thrust beneath their feathers, already roosted. The hounds hesitated at the door, until Dutchess invited two with her voice and her fingers, crooking her elbow, to bring her favorites, Cinco and Spook. They slunk on their bellies, and huddled down at her feet when she sat in her mother's chair. She raised the sewing in her hands. She wanted to study the patterns and hold the bone needles. She realized she'd not yet lit the candles; only the lantern was burning. She could see nothing, as the moon began to rise, but the shape of the leather, her own lap and knees, and the two hounds gathered at her feet.

Dutchess lit five candles from the lantern wick. She turned a few coals in the fireplace and they smoldered. Five lights flickered about her when she sat down, like birds flared from branches or stars returning to heaven: an assumption of light bodies. She looked at her own spread fingers on the pattern; for her fingers lay flared, as though her body could barely restrain an outward movement. She studied the threaded designs in the leather. She touched the threads, and felt them out with five fingers. She took the pressure of threads, and she held the bone needles, while she imagined: a dark animal burns like a ship on grassland; its body flares into clouds of fire and smoke, high sails to bear the body on; a slender man flees, his back visible in departure.

Startled, Dutchess dropped the leather, and the

bone needles bounced, sprung, and rattled on the cabin floor, startling the hounds. She forgot the fire, which needed wood. She covered herself in some old buffalo robes, then slept in the increasing cold, while the moon rose, and she dreamed things she wouldn't remember. The hounds, as the spring night mounted, lay with their long noses across her feet, and occasionally shook in their sleep, as if they shared her dreams.

IT'S MORNING AND BY THE TIME SHE arrives, bruised by her plunge through mountains, into the silence of the fire where three hunters linger at coffee, she's already moved, through an involved progress, from her fit by the river to her peculiar madness. She's like a child, and there's nothing beyond her awareness: even the landscape has entered her obsession, even these men by the fire she comes to suddenly, descending out of a cloud. She tells them the name that a whiteman, a Frenchman like them, once gave her, *Marie;* and she speaks to these men in their own tongue, slowly mouths now strange French words she needs for her story.

Sawpootway or Marie came from above them, around a gorse bush, after descending the draw through the misty cloud, down through the pines, among silver-trunked aspens. She knew the three hunters from previous seasons. They didn't hear her till she stood among them and spoke her name, Marie, the name she brought from her grief. She couldn't remember their names. No one of them had ever spoken much to her before, nor had they known her by any name but *the squaw*. They'd been, like other hunters and trappers, reminders of the world outside mountains. Berrigan, with his air of casual intimacy, kept them at a distance while they traded. So it seems to her now. Did she learn her distrust of Legget from his own of other men, of those who came from the settlements, like invaders, with news of that greater world? Or, more likely, did Berrigan, holding that world away from them, only express her own will? She stares through the men at the fire, and doesn't care how they consider her; she sees through their stares.

Now, finding the speech of their tongue with some pain, she asks if they've seen Berrigan or Dutch, if they've seen the trapper, Legget. She says she's tried to track them, but their spoor has risen into air like birds. The men say they know them, but haven't seen anyone. Their words seem part of her body, as if the men speak within her will.

When she tells them what happened, they don't believe her; but they'll tell each other her story over other campfires, over other coffees. They will tell how she appears to them, ragged, torn from the mist like a scrap from their cold mountain dreams, torn from the cloud that's like a halo of tears she doesn't weep; how she arrives so stern and upright among them, calling herself by name as if they don't know who she is without the name, as the smoke rises through the aspens; how she speaks in their tongue to tell her strange story of impersonation. They will make it all a campfire joke, telling how her son appeared to Legget like a woman in love, how Legget and the son disappeared in their violent elopement. And they will elaborate the joke in a few new ears, till others, who will never have seen her descending mountains, will take it as their own and stretch the simple tale into an even more ludicrous jest—including the pathos of the mother looking for her lost son, Berrigan's own search imagined as a comic underpinning and relief to the great joke and counter-joke of disguise and theft.

Marie doesn't mention her daughter left in the valley. She's forgotten Dutchess, the girl consumed in the image of lost Dutch; until the three men remember Legget's desire and remember the girl in his desire. They remind Marie that the girl still exists, after all. Perhaps *there's* something to hold onto; or something to release herself from, if she's to be successful in her search. She decides she must cut herself away from that reminder, leaving these men swiftly; for the men remember that Dutchess must be somewhere and they can imagine how she must figure in the tale they will elaborate, how they'll tell of the daughter, significantly unmentioned by the mother. Marie imagines they will scarcely mention the girl at first, but each will invent a role for Dutchess in the story, each role essentially the same, almost all unconscious, understood without speech; then, within interstices, crude jests will arise of Dutchess's singleness, her unmentionableness, foul tales of candles and hounds, of cocks and hens. But it will not begin in crudeness:

Dutchess will come, down to the family banquet, at dinner time. No one will be there. Hounds will sniff at her father's chair. She'll call out. She must call or no one will ever come. She must call directly, to have her chance. "Who is there?" She'll hear no answer, though the hounds will eagerly cock their heads. She'll sit in her father's chair and light the candles, unable to call any more, all her human breath used up in the single question. The tiny flames of the candles, flickering, will make her sleepy, hissing through air as she nods her head. Dutchess will dream of her lost brother, her father, her wandering mother; then another man will move in the dream, disappearing on muleback, and she'll wake to see the candles, flames like bird wings above the table. As she leans back and waits, without speech, for a husband, worms will rise from the damp earth, like roots, and become tall hunters with shiny blue guns, before the mountain slaps them back into the lower ground, the white horns turning red like the candle flames. Then the hunters will speak their cruel jests from the earth, muttering while she waits for a husband, who hasn't come, who she doesn't believe in.

For a long time it is all these men will feel of her, speaking inaudibly to no one in particular, not even to themselves. They speak into the face of their dreams, dreams they don't pretend to understand any more, dreams no longer their own, speaking nothing really aloud for other ears except the crudest jests and that one cry of hers, sudden in their tale, as if from their sleep: "Who is there?" Only the large man, who speaks most to Marie, will feel any differently about Dutchess that day, after Marie departs. Marie's not very sure what these men will do or imagine and she's frightened of them: the more she feels she's entered their imagination, their wills, the more she feels they escape her conception into their own lives.

Will they tell anyone, except wives perhaps, if they ever have them: that they, meaning only to jest in the misery of other lives, once invented someone to love, a young woman they might come to, a tall, dark girl they'd seen only from a distance, while bartering with Berrigan, a young woman who, they begin to feel, always expected them? Will their jests become the way they take her curse off themselves, the damnation of having conceived someone they could have loved?

Who are such men? She still can't remember their names. One of the three, who speaks most, whose head looms as if it came always from shadows—head large like a buffalo's, a bear's, or an elephant's, moving like the top of a broad-leafed cottonwood—reminds her of someone she shouldn't have forgotten. The other two are smaller: in the firelight and dawn, almost interchangeable figures, slight and flexible, informed by their campfire, a light like a bush on fire in the depths of each pair of eyes. One's hair seems both red and blue; the other's red and silver. The first is alert for danger like a fox; the second as careless as a fish: both seem elusive, as if, when she trapped them, they could escape into each other, or into the landscape. The three remind her of something that died in her before she came to the valley.

When Marie goes, they haven't fully escaped her, madness and three heads weave together, and hands slap thighs and shoulders. She had coffee with them, talked long, repeating herself, then departed swiftly, to make up the lost time of speech, downward through mountains, through the aspen level before rising again through aspen, pine, and rocks. She left them among preliminary improvisations of their jest. They laugh over last cups before they rise from their morning fire, scuff dirt over flames with their boots, pour on remains of coffee, till the fire smothers, the last tail of white smoke coming up through poured earth and liquid. The large hunter sneezes, and his great frame shakes.

He walks, his shaggy head weaving, as a tree might walk, toward the horses tied under the light-green aspen trees. The mules are also hobbled there; the other men approach them. The large man talks to the horses, tells of the woman's story, in the metaphors of horses' needs. No one else can hear him. He feels the horses understand him as a woman might, and he's always handled horses, catered to their needs, even these obscure ones shadowed under the budding aspens, his hands on their withers, on the arched necks, the flinching nostrils, his fingers on the reins and saddles; and he looks at the trees, the wood extended and full, and slender, like the arms of women. He prepares the horses for the day, working in the shadow of those trees. The other two men pack the mules, with less attention; but the large man loves the mules as he does the horses, if not more, as though, as he looks at mules, they acquire a religious significance he's just learning. He would handle them himself, if he didn't want to provide something to do for the others, but the animals belong to his world.

When they're ready to go out from the camp, the three ride as Marie watches from above, into old conceptions of themselves, as if they exist in an earlier time, as if the story the woman told had entered their past and they followed. The large man, his head nodding, with the rhythm of the horse, above the bay's peaked ears, realizes that Marie is the one he might have loved, that all he's felt of the girl is more true of the girl's mother, if he'd just noticed her among them, the woman both beautiful and young, full of her pursuit, stern in her grief, as if she appeared to them, at the campfire, out of that other, earlier life of his own, out of an existence he's somehow missed, unluckily, while some other lives out that life for him. He searches the rocks for her, but she's gone on. He sees the other two men divide around a dead bear's skeleton. This man passes a hand over his eyes, then a cloud, as if of memory, dissipates, before his face, like a dream that might have repeated itself. He sighs, and rides by the animal's death.

IN AVALANCHE—LIKE TREE BOUGHS, OF twigs and buds, falling down their trunk—a mountain descends in its snow; like fire, huge white buds burst, to bloom through individual pines and aspens, spuming snow cast up like bird wings, as Marie descends at the breaking-up, her hands stained from berries lately picked and eaten. In her body, running is no strain below that snow slide, as she runs down from berry-picking in the high gorge among signs of bear, her body smoothed down the grassy slope, among the hard rocks jutting, to the river where she becomes entirely free of the danger of snow, still moving down through high trees, as the smoke of snow rises and collects, like the treetops in a grove of cottonwood she knew in childhood, like cloudbreath, puffs, like the heads of animals looming from low bodies.

She isn't afraid of the snow slide now. In her fear she saw her daughter bending over a dish of water and Marie nodded to the young face, where pebbles, like trout eyes, a sparkling ore, clouded her reflection, ripples waving like feathers.

Birds flooded from the groves, from pine and aspen, over Marie's head and over the water; they were the dark advance wave of the avalanche; they came from the fire to reform their own cloud in the clear sky beyond the river.

But Marie is no longer afraid, she's safe, she scoops cold water and drinks; she sucks upon pebbles, as she did as a child in her father's tribe. She feels, as she has for twenty years, that she's the only one left of her tribe, her children become white people like their father; she's lost them in Dutch's loss. The animals from the mountain, increasing, flee to the water, unafraid of the woman who kneels and ignores them. They swarm from the trees, unidentified and undifferentiated animals swimming over the thin, growing river. Marie drinks beyond their panic, and she sees the bottom of the water, beyond the reflection of her face and beyond the fish that make clouds with active fins. She sees frogs rising from tadpoles; the world departs from her. For this instant, she no longer exists, driven so far by the falling snow, cast out of herself, after the world vanished in her son.

Dutchess, as though she has nothing to do with her mother who kneels at the river, and sees her (in real water this time), bends to her labor. She keeps the house while she's waiting for a husband. Her straw broom, bound by leather on a branch, sweeps over the toes of her own bare feet. The day grows warm in proportion to her work, from the cold morning. Dutchess lingers over each physical moment, as if she wishes no instant of time to escape her body's awareness. So she works in the house while Marie rises and follows the water, as if the river were the escaping world, and Marie goes in gullies and ravines, closer each sunrise and sunset to her old home on the plains.

Eventually the mountains dwindle, the river widens; a reluctance holds her back, on the rim, from the badlands she can see to the east. Her life, in these years, has become confined to mountains, bound in rocks like a demon of her tribe's religion. Her father said giant rock demons from these mountains would ride down at the end of time, terrible things, animal and man combined, riding themselves, riding their bodies out of where-the-earth-sleeps, from the hidden places. In death, her people took the journey of duels to these mountains, to live again, where-the-earth-sleeps, where she'd already lived so long with Berrigan; she took him there.

For hours she's held on the rim of rocks, suspended, still feels the world escaped her down the river, and she can't control anything in her life. All moves beyond her. She feels she's even lost her home in the valley. An image of Dutchess rises strongly, then fades gradually as though eroded by time and distance; then there's no pain, the ligaments weakened, her daughter fading beyond her, as if from the present into the lost past, into a life her mother doesn't know.

Dutchess, behind the chicken house, has a garden to plant, to keep the valley's seasonal life going, and she will, if the cock and hounds allow her, if they stay out of her way. She bends with a stick to the bean rows Berrigan has plowed and left unplanted. In the harvest, if no one ever returns, she plans to trade goods, such as these beans, to the hunters and trappers, to the few scattered men who've come the past two years. She will deal with them, she thinks, just as her father did, taking the food up the valley to men like the ones Marie met recently, the three now approaching the valley in a roundabout way, as though they're reluctant to meet Dutchess.

She feels the influence of her mother has controlled her all the time she's been alone here, as if she were only an extension of the mother, repeating her mother's daily acts; her mother would have planted these beans. Now Dutchess's eyes would peer into the bean holes she pierces, as into her future, divining; her green stick would disappear into holes like a serpent;

everything, if she has her first wish, would return to its origin, like fathers and mothers reversing to children, and time would get still, she supposes, like a child in the seed before kicking, and all would be home again. At the sound of a voice calling for anyone present, she looks up from her probing, and sees a man come around the chicken shed; the birds peck again when he's passed them.

The man wears large, furry mittens on his hands. She wonders if he'll be her husband. She thought, at first, he was her father, but he hasn't her father's smile. Then she wondered if she imagined him; he wasn't real yet. This man glowers and looks at his wrapped hands, as if they've swollen in hurt. When he's come nearer, Dutchess saw, he's carrying something in those big hands. She couldn't see what yet. He comes from another world and time. She doesn't know where she is, whether this happened to her before or might happen yet; then she thinks he's real after all, in the same world she is, bringing her something in his hands. Why is he wearing mittens? Are his hands cold? Does he protect them from whatever he bears within them?

Dutchess began to come to herself, as if freed from her mother's touch, placed upon her in birth or imprinted in conception, and she saw the man resembled her father in size. The man isn't clear, yet hasn't quite entered her life. She wondered if she would let him come. She raised the stick above her waist, both hands clenched upon it, and tugged as though she'd spread it over her breasts, in extra covering and protection. She thought she saw, in his hands, black bird wings and the fins of trout, all brilliant as if these parts would stir to independent life, like flames on a distant mountainside, fire her mother could survive but she could not. The man says her father sent him. In those words he came clear to her; the day rolled back on itself, the man clearer, but not so near yet as she'd thought he was. She thought she should be thinking about her mother, but she wasn't.

The man, Joseph Adams, nudged the rooster aside with his boot, and he scuffed his way through the chickens. He seemed to have no horse for this journey, nor any mule; apparently he came alone, on foot, into the valley, a pack like a hump on his shoulders. Dutchess, holding the green stick clenched before her, suddenly dropped it.

In flesh, she thought he was even larger than Berrigan, like puffy dough risen, suppressed only by the pack's pressure. His nose was a knob, and his hands were clothed thickly, like clubs, as though they were injured and bandaged.

He removed his pack when he saw the girl staring, when she'd dropped her stick, and he set his burden upon the plowed ground. He found something in his hands. He paused and stared, as though he'd forgotten it was there. Then he took it toward her carefully, as if it were the one thing his gloves were meant to protect him from.

Dutchess watched him come. She hadn't said a word to him. She stared at his hands in momentary fear. He still seemed to study the hunk of bark he brought, holding it clear of his body, walking. As her fear eased, wings and fins became the bark torn from the tree, borne by a man risen from her daydreams. When he arrived, she held out her hands.

Adams gave her the wood. He said her father sent him, to bring the wood to her mother. Adams said he'd thought the mother would be there. Dutchess stared at the bark, without answering him. She couldn't read the Indian markings on the strip's interior side, though they, or others like them, were familiar to her from her mother's sewing. It would have been, she knew, a reassuring message for her mother, a sign to say all was in order in the world; but it only disconcerted Dutchess. Adams was saying his name. He said she didn't know him, but he'd known her father last year. He said he guessed she'd never seen him before. Her mother hadn't seen him, only Berrigan and Dutch. He seemed embarrassed.

She held the marked, white side of the wood to him, and asked if he knew what it said.

No, Berrigan didn't tell him, but he supposed it was about her brother, whom her father'd been looking for, and it might say something about the man named Legget.

Dutchess asked if he knew what it was all about, if he knew why she was alone here.

But Adams knew only that Berrigan had said he was looking for Legget and Dutch. He hadn't heard anything about her mother. Was she gone?

Dutchess nodded. They stood near each other to study the marks in the wood that Dutchess held: there was something like a snake; there was a four-legged animal that looked like a deer or goat; then her father's knife had described what appeared to be a bear; a buffalo; an eagle; a horse with long ears more like a rabbit's ears or a mule's; then something like a child, misshapen, with a tail; and a naked man with wavy lines gouged around him like scars or heat devils, like the snake shapes her mother had often fixed in patterns. It was the first time Dutchess was aware she wished to know what her mother's designs meant, if they really meant anything other than themselves; she'd learned, early from her mother's mouth, only the spoken language of the tribe. Now it seemed to her that her parents had kept the secret of this visible language, intentionally, though she'd never asked anyone to explain the signs. The pictures seemed more like acts than words with meanings; it was difficult for her to think of them as anything like language.

Adams said he guessed her father didn't want to write in words. If Berrigan had, Adams said he could have read some of them for her; for he knew some words.

Dutchess said she could have read them herself; her father taught both her and her brother.

Or, Adams said, if Berrigan had wanted, he could have told Adams what to say. That would have made most sense. Adams screwed up his eyes at the signs, over her shoulder, in an effort to understand Berrigan's intention in writing in wood.

Dutchess said this was something special for her mother.

Adams asked where the woman was.

Dutchess said she'd gone, days before, to the river with her father, and with Dutch.

She must have gone to look for them, Adams guessed.

As though they realized that what they said meant less and less, was less their language than another communication, they gradually became silent. Dutchess poked her stick about, making random holes she didn't intend to plant beans in. The holes were deep enough, but she kept the seed in her pocket. Adams stared at her feet, at the holes, at the moving stick. She said he must be hungry, coming so far. Almost whispering, she said he should come up to the house, said it casually though, as if she'd known him as well as her father or brother.

He said he was mostly tired.

So they walked together to the house, his gloved hands and her bared ones clenched behind their backs. Adams had raised his pack onto his shoulders again, shrugging it into place between the blades. The four hounds followed them slowly; the rooster flew up to the sodded roof, and tucked his head under his wings. She saw his sorrel horse tied to the cottonwood.

They didn't speak as they walked. Up the long valley, Adams saw the two-peaked mountain rise between other mountains. They walked slowly as if they were hesitant, afraid, to intrude on their shadows moving ahead of them in the afternoon. They entered the house, without the hounds. Dutchess told Adams to take off his boots. She'd bring him hot water; she said it was something her father liked. Embarrassed, in sweaty socks, he sat down in the mother's chair, by the sewing on a small table. Dutchess disappeared behind a blanket hung to curtain off the house.

He moved his hands from the mittens carefully, as he'd remove bandages, and he looked long at his hands, as though he'd never seen them, white and pink and pulpy, padded with calluses that seemed unnatural. He laid the big mittens on the stitched designs he didn't notice, and he stretched his fingers toward the fire in the south wall. Dutchess reappeared to hang a pot of water. She sat on the floor, to watch at the fire. Adams watched her, the dark stretch of her neck before the fire. He knew he was waiting for something to happen, something surprising she'd do, but he couldn't imagine anything beyond her present still figure. He watched her back, and felt a peculiar peace in that lingering study—their long silence—unexpectedly comforting to the trapper, the hunter, Adams.

Adams woke with a slight jerk, the girl put a basin of hot water before his feet. He smelled an odor that might have been the smell of his feet or of food.

Dutchess knelt: Berrigan rubs his eyes, wiping mist away, and peers into water as if searching for fish; his feet feel damp, like his head, cold like all his extremities. When he walks away, rising from water, he hears a sound like ice breaking up in his body.

Dutchess stood straight, leaving the basin. She didn't know what to do with her hands; they became jerky on her wrists; her elbows and fingers crooked nervously. Adams slowly removed his heavy socks, flexed his great toes in the steam, and let his feet settle gradually down into hot water. His mouth flinched upward, and his eyes crinkled, as if he smiled at her. Then his feet settled, toes like stilled fish on the bottom. The water went smooth as his face.

Adams reposed, still embarrassed but more easy, in Berrigan's house, seated before the tall girl whose wide mouth raised toward him. Adams shut his eyes and almost slipped back to sleep above her smile, but she startled him: he feigned a sleep and felt her hands move, her fingers under his feet, caressing his soles, and he felt her press the sides, the firm indentation of her thumbs. Adams slitted his eyes to see her kneeling at the basin; she was looking down toward his feet in her hands, as if she peered into her reflected face. That was his surprise, he thought, this unforeseen washing, her touch. He moved his toes, slightly as in sleep, to draw her eyes; her fingers moved down and came to his toes under water. He became still to her touch, relinquishing all past efforts to overcome things. He felt he could live without desire; he might stay so forever.

But Dutchess took advantage of what she took to be his sleep, to say she'd been so lonely for them, for father and brother, mother, so . . .

And Adams opened his eyes, ended that pretense of sleep, and leaned forward to place his bared fingers in her hair. Her startled eyes became as still as his toes had been to her fingers. When he'd tangled his fingers in her hair, he pulled back her head so her face would rise. He was the one surprised when he kissed her. He felt the stillness of her fingers on his toes. He felt her lips swelling.

Dutchess closed her eyes and her father, Orcus Berrigan, stands knee-deep in water between the waterfall and the rock face, his back pressed to the damp rock wall; and the roar sounds outside the water. He's still, waits for someone to come behind the screen, in to him; he gathers courage to plunge out through the falling water, to appear so suddenly, in mid-air arched like a trout toward someone below him. He flattens against the wall and imagines fire slides, down a mountainside, like burial earth, but white like an avalanche, a long animal growing, moving sleekly, low to the earth, the body of the beast rolled above itself like a white shadow thrown upon the sky. Dutchess placed her wet fingers in Adams's hair. She kissed him blindly; she didn't wish to see who he was. She kissed without thinking she'd never known how to kiss him.

Adams, leaning forward, lifting her above the basin, still kissed the girl. For an instant, she'd shied, as if startled to find that someone else existed in the kiss. She let her length bend to him, like a bow unstrung.

Dutchess heard Adams say words in her ear she

couldn't understand, like the signs from her father to her mother, those animal figures.

Adams smelled the cooking on the fire, the odor of chicken. He felt her thumb probe gently in one ear; her palm cupped the other. His blood curled back fiercely, resounding in him.

Later, she wouldn't weep, to hear her own blood, the sound of her desire rising in her ears, as if what they did was something heard, like the voice of a stranger in the room and the bed, when Adams became familiar to her.

MARIE DREAMED, IN THE EARLY MORN-ing: Dutchess appears as if from the past, turns and becomes her mother, Marie departing as though she left her own sleeping, her dreaming body behind. Startled, she woke and rushed into the day. Tiring later, she slowed gradually as though something more than fear held her back. The desperation of her effort, to find her son, entered her like a cloud, a foreboding mist inside her chest, a pressure, her lungs became that cloud, the vapor of constrained breath that adhered to her interior with so much weight, any way she moved. Then, as she walked early in that day, she dreamed her menfolk more than she pursued them.

Or she sat, as now (for what's past is past), to images that appear when she looks up from her toes; for under an opposing pine, a man sits blackly in the patch of snow, his knees pulled high to his chest and grasped in thin arms; his hat brim, which once was stiff, leans down upon his eyes. His pose is stiff. She doesn't yet believe in him; he's not quite there for her yet.

He isn't sleeping. Sometimes he appears to glance up at Marie, about to rise and approach her. But they sit so long that she dozes off, lightly, and dreams of another man: I'm red-headed, blue-eyed, sitting in a fish mouth, as in a room I've furnished long before to my desire.

The man under the pine, outside the dream, watches her; he would like to penetrate the dream. While she sleeps, he rises, to begin the labor he'll adore and hate. Under the hat brim his face sets darkly, as if sooted, where points of his white teeth glitter. He crouches in the old, hard snow and, with raw hands, chops, breaks pieces of hard crust, lifting the fragments by their jagged edges, the severe white breakage without thaw, his bare hands raw and glowing. He enters the spirit of his work, like a stubbornness set against her impenetrable dream, against her sleep he thinks excludes him.

With immaculate care, the man, unseen by Marie but moved as though moved by her hand, constructs objects that are significant to him: a wife he's never had; his three unborn children, of sexes undetermined. He is never quite done, the project of snow endless, the unfinished, experimental life of construction. He works on at his family figure, arranging the teeth of snow, like precise flames set in the tree's shadow.

So Marie wakes to find him before her, sweating as if the liquid of his flesh were his newest growth, latest ring of tree bark, his hands flapping, rapid, fanning the rough edges, his mouth gasping open like the gill of a landed fish or a bellows to the snow. He feels desperate in the knowledge of hard fragments melting, eventually. Now, perhaps something of what he wants would stand, if he'd leave his figures alone, move beyond anxiety to transform, not be so like an industrious angel, busy, past recall of the moment and shape. His arms flail uselessly and overheat his body. He wishes something would interrupt him, end this figure-making, his horror.

Marie stands, shakily, and wobbles to him. She would fall if he weren't present to embarrass her; now she believes in his existence, growing urgent in her, like a child. For the moment, she's forgotten what she'd be urged to. She stumbles, unable to understand why or how she walks, her whole experience come to this misunderstanding. Unwatched by her, the son's, the husband's images turn within, revolving; and they wake. Till now, she hasn't yet seen them in the full reality of absence, just as her children once pulsed to her blood before she knew they lived in her body, stirred in her before any knowledge of them. So the images of her lost son and husband worked.

She doesn't understand the growth of those images within her, nor her own insistence on walking, hungry and weak, toward the unfamiliar man among his family figures. She knows growth only as that urgency she thinks her own. Come to the stranger's distorted figures, she bends to a snow child, to a ragged creature, sharp-edged and cold to her fingers, so cold it seems closed to her touch. She bends, careful of cutting herself. She raises one piece of one child-shape, to her mouth, and she nibbles on what might be a finger; she sucks as if it's her own mothering grief she eats. Greedy, she shatters the figure to fragments, fallen sharply from her old age's life, from her future like bones of her love, these white icy needles to stitch her death's pattern. She eats, hungrily, all that child of snow, as if it's the meat of some animal she picks from the ground.

The man watches, in sympathy with her hunger. He doesn't mind her eating up his experiment in a snow family; now it's what they seem to exist for, and he's resigned. She's relieved him of the burden of creating them. They speak then.

Between children of snow, Marie, in English, asks him his name.

He says it's Thurlow. Then he says it is John Leger Thurlow, the reverend.

She asks which name is his. She doesn't understand.

Thurlow, unsurprised, says it is both, all. He watches her eat, without care for familiar lives he imagined; but he will not eat with her yet, and will never eat of that snow.

When she tells him her story, as if he asked for it, the story's fragmentary, between bites, like the figures she eats, like the crusty, broken snow. Thurlow interrupts to say he's doing nothing now but preaching to ice and snow, or to the thaw.

Marie, telling the story, remembers her son; she wants him back. When Thurlow asks for a description, to identify the boy, she says he is like something she can't remember. She says her husband was once like a buffalo, a bear, something else.

Thurlow says she must miss him; but she says no, she can't remember well enough. Thurlow says he knows places to look for the husband and son, crevices men might hide in, lakes like clear fingers, where they might float safely under a mountain. Marie tells him she's grateful to him, and he, eagerly, speaks of some of those places, as he strides around her, his hands clasped behind his back, his head down and shoulder blades sticking up and out, while she listens and eats more of the third child, her body filling with the white hard snow.

Once, as he moves unseen behind her, Thurlow kneels briefly, dipping his knees down swiftly, to the image of his wife. In this instant, his eyes become like trout eyes, as if, with only a faint white glimmer, he looks on the snow from his death, peers from the great distance into this alien world as a fish peers through his watery medium. His fingers play on the rough edges he imagined his love in.

Embarrassed, Thurlow rises; but Marie, intent on her eating, didn't even see him kneel. He thrusts his red hands into the pockets of a thin black coat, and his eyes become the tired, blooded eyes of a man, as they've never quite been before, as though the eyes blossomed now from the interior, where his images of family came from. He remains by the image of his wife and, when Marie turns toward him full of his imagined children, Thurlow's eyes swim toward her slowly, as if to enter her, to his children, and transform them with his fatherly presence. He glances at the remaining snow image and casually lifts one large piece of rough snow from his wife and breaks it over his knee. Fragments fall down, like broken pine needles come to dust from the trees, disintegrated bodies moting the sunlight. Marie steps from the image's shadow, from the fragments of childish snow bodies littering the ground at her feet, from the marks her feet tore in the crust while she ate. Fragments still fall from Thurlow's hands, while his eyes are closed, and he imagines snow falling from the boughs of pine trees as something climbs up them. Then he opens his eyes and takes a large piece of the image in each hand. He slides each into a pocket of his coat, where he warmed his hands before. He speaks, to say it's so she'll be able to eat another time. So if she's ready, full now, shall they go?

His voice has acquired a new urgency, apart from her idea of him; Thurlow hears the tiniest sounds of the mountain; it preaches to him, gently, like creaking bones, as if someone begins to move, gigantically toward him, as yet invisible, almost still risings. He hears Marie repeatedly tell him that she's grateful for help.

So they begin. They ascend the slope of a flat-topped mountain, not so high a mountain as others. They waver up the slope, and seek sure footing together. They go arm in arm, their steps falling behind them, sharp breaks through the crust, like a staggering signature of their climb, as if Marie designs their way crookedly.

Once, as they pause in ascent, Thurlow removes his dark hat to mop his brow. He breathes harshly in the thin air. Marie, leaning on a stripped, straight bough that Thurlow cut her, sees his head shining, the round, bony dome of skull reflect the sun, as though light enters a pool. His ears poise themselves stiffly against soft cushions of hair at his temples.

Thurlow settles his hat back again, lines the brim up with his brows, two patches of hair over his eyes that the bared skull disappears above. He pulls his shoulders toward each other, as if he'd cross them on his chest. The blades spread behind him, rising toward his neck. Hunched forward, he begins to move, and she follows. He looks back and sees her long aspen crutch, piercing dark holes in the crust, those definitive markings of the pole in snow, as if she wished to make sure, beyond the marks of their feet, that someone could track them.

THE LONG PLATEAU BEGINS GREEN AT the rim: the snow piles up the center nightly from the vegetable edge, from the tree ring, the spruce and pine. Marie and Thurlow don't try to pass the white cone, circle instead two days till they arrive at the opposite side and a vision of the long green valleys westward, like rivers run down from this snow plateau. When Thurlow was discovered, Marie turned back from the rim of the mountains, away from the eastern plains that loomed again, as in younger days, like something more than mountains, higher than mountains in her dreams. Now she points to the crooked valleys beneath them, and says that somewhere there are lakes. Thurlow agrees; she points to places the clouds descend toward, dipping, watery, and clouds point, like her finger does, at lakes curled as if in sleep, quiet long bodies of water hiding fish deep.

Before descent, they make camp above the valleys, green and like fingers outstretched, relaxed. They eat only the herbiage Marie found among the trees at the plateau's edge: tiny blue berries, thin brown vines, the dark purple leaves. All the snow in Thurlow's pockets leaves a damp coldness. They sit within the lean-to Thurlow made of boughs, upon the spruce boughs they'll soon sleep on. Marie nibbles bits of the plants, as he does. She doesn't understand how Thurlow, having lost his mule, survived before she found him, and she believes he didn't exist then, believes she knows his life is only what she'll give him, in this time of travel; believes, though she knows she's mad.

For liquid they have the snow of the plateau melted in the hands and mouth and stomach, refresh-

ing before their sleep. Thurlow removes his hat before the fire, as the sun's last light reflects from the
snowbank behind them. In the bared skin, Marie
studies the clear outline of his skull, no marks on his
revealed flesh but interior signs; his skin almost irre-
sistible to the knife she hid in her dress for Legget.
She feels she could peel his head like a round fruit, so
ripe on his body, as if on a pear bough; then the white
skin would fall down about his feet to contain his
toes, his heels; or she could sign that skin, for him,
shape that flesh from without, as the bone shapes it
from within, make her markings of animals upon the
white skin gleaming with more potential than snow,
cut the formal designs, her message for whoever may
meet him after her. And he wouldn't forget her, and
would move to her rhythm. Her signs might maintain
him when she's gone. Then he might live after; he
couldn't otherwise.

Yet her hand doesn't follow that notion, and her
activity removes inward near Thurlow's nodding
sleep, at sunset, near the quirks of dream his eyelids
indicate. Though her own eyes remain open, her
body's surface extended toward him in the line of her
sight, all behind her eyes sinks, toward her lungs and
heart, toward that interior life, all that heaviness, the
pressure down, strains against the horizontal line of
her outward vision. So she stares at Thurlow as
blankly as an animal might: within herself, she fades,
as though fainting, toward the earth, sinks into her
bowels.

So far descended, Marie feels she'll come to her
boy, find him and revive him, as though he drowned.
They'll go home together. She knows she is, for this
duration, still mad in grief, but she believes. She sinks
so, as if into that old winter, the past cold, taking on

all that grave pressure that bears her downward. She grows expectant then in sinking, unrepentant in the pleasant weakness, as if she thawed after all into summer heat, not back to cold winter, going into an ecstasy in the loins that become heavier than her whole former body. Thurlow, that comfortable presence, nods in sleep, Thurlow, like a good companion she improvised from her love for her son. Her conversation with the world is inaudible, the quiet slow and deep inside her. She feels her descent, like a departure she's not sure she wants. In a time without extension, with no movement outward except the blind line of her stare (which still moves toward him as if an avalanche, against the usual grain of fall, slid sideways to soothe a mountainous sorrow); suddenly, after so much falling, her descending movement coincides with her sight, as though she now found Thurlow's sunstruck head, discovered him, the gleam in her womb. Who is Thurlow? She asks him, and the bald head gleams with the fire and the sun off the snowbank.

His bald head replies, in the oblique light, flashing its message while he sleeps, that he's preached, most recently, only to mountains, has told them to abide her coming, to become still to her, for his sake too. The domed head sighs and flashes again as though that were his sermon; then she hears only snores of Thurlow's sleep, his breath rough through his mouth; for her eyes swallow all the light as she consumes now: his bare head, the snowbank, the fire of coals outside the shelter, that setting sun. Marie tells the mountains to quiet, that she hears something new stir within Thurlow's domed skull, the head now within her. She hears, as an infinitesimal clapping, such as bird wings or fish fins might sound, her invisible son begin in Thurlow's absorbed head, the boy as small as a fish egg.

Almost imperceptibly, Dutch rises from the stream of beginning-again, where nothing is yet made, within her heart's beat and heaviness, like the word silence says, as though dark particles of earth stirred in the slow growth of black pine roots, disturbing, in the thaw of mountains. Dutch lives in her sigh, began again, as in the tenuous applause of angels or stars, tremblings in the distance, as if a scale gestures on a fish whose scales are all eggs, as Dutch seeks his life beyond the fish and, within a lake that's like Thurlow's skull, will break away, like the scale, from that cold-blooded body into improbable new life, as if a juggled orange shall leap from a juggler's fingers, before his fingers move.

Marie feels the internal pressure of Thurlow's domed head, feels it as her son's medium, knows his tiny movement within her, joyed under Thurlow's hairless skin. She feels full of heat, melted down, and his skull is like a nested egg, she like the setting hen, till she feels a needed change, a transfer, as in a dream, the small life from skull to crooked lake. She feels interior pricks of his life, as if, under the lake, the sun will revolve like Thurlow's head, turn belly down, and will swim pale, translucent, like the skull skin, while blue veins throb. It's all confused, been confused in many images; she finds a clarity in the future: from Dutch's side, arms will come slowly like tentacles or antennae or vines, probing out the clear water, making a surface in the roomy place. So his blood will warm in the icy lake, among the fish who knew him intimately. She feels they've been there, mother and son, before, in the water more natural than the heat of Thurlow's head. Then, in that future, fish will look upon what's become stranger to them than their familiar bodies: looking back, into and through their eyes, Dutch will peer, to an ancient world like the sky, and he'll know the fish don't see him, except as a mote in the stream they swim through, a fleck in their medium; for they'll see through his new, human body, as through a lens, toward what he grows to, and to them he'll be like something swimming in his mother's eyes; those fish will look toward another thing not quite human, like the angels she imagined, or starlike birds that flutter; and it will seem gills darken to wings in his sides, his arms probing *their* water and *her* eyes, his fingers soon to surface, as though he'd add flesh to angels, pure spirits before, and fling birds to completing death, as though the transformation of angels and birds, become mortal or finished in his growth, sealed all creatures, the animals, into his new life, joined in love previously unknown, when lips suck on teeth and a tongue explores the air in a lover's mouth.

Marie believes: becoming visible, Dutch will rise, unrecognized at first but as a gentle probing of her body, strange in the beginnings, as though a fish is thrown out of his place in the water, into her eyes.

Thurlow nods to the fire, the sun down, the horizon orange, as the boy's life freshens in Marie. Now she closes her eyes, she sleeps; while Thurlow, eyelids twitching, dreams of her belly, a roundness there, then dreams of imaginary children; then the imagined wife. Pain enters him in sleep, as if her belly rose, through his imaginary family, into his ears, like a sound he's heard for the first time, a voice he might recognize soon. When he wakes, his sleep will seem strange to him, as though it belongs to another.

THURLOW COMES FROM FAR UNDER: HE wakes from dreams that entangle him like long fingers curled in his beard. He would sleep more, instead of rising, and would hold dear those dreams that won't linger in waking: he'd be tangled in streaming ferns, be choked on the lake bottom. He wouldn't lift his head and see Marie eating the small roots, nor would he feel the white dawn break on his eyelids, the day come cold as his feet, while his toes are still as if in dream, his blood crackling as he stands. He wouldn't run stiff fingers through the frost-hoary beard, to comb it for this day as he does. No, Thurlow wonders why he's here, leaning toward her, over the fire she revives with her breath and hands. He wonders why he's come upon her, when he's feeling so wintry and alone, as if he'd never thaw past a lake's shielding ice, as if he'd lie still in his dreams. The air stands, a glass between them, preventing him, and now, as he's changed by desire, it's that mirror of glass he leans toward, wishing to see himself, and yet to move, eyes clearing, through the mirror, cold membrane of air, to some warmth with her, so that their chief communication won't have been through the snow he built figures of, snow that melted or she consumed. He wonders how he changed to want to be so near her.

Thurlow walks behind a tall shrub, but won't piss, release his flow, at first, for fear his liquid turned, within the night, to ice, might break him. At last he manages, staining the snow, the steam rises; he puts his cock away and steps out, creaking forward. He revolves his hat on his head slowly, as though to wind himself back into dreaming, under the ice; there his mind still holds the temperature of deep water, where he's still, untempted, by the external vision, of Marie, beyond him, through the air. For the last time, he's able to feel resentment fully, that she's roused him out of his cold self. He blows on his hands and squats a little distance from the fire; then he stands, he walks around Marie and the flames she kneels to. He feels her person and the fire rising.

Thurlow sees how she looks at him, impatiently. She stands. They move, to go down the flat mountain, without breaking their fast with anything more than the snow and the dark, curled roots, small themselves and matted with tiny hairs. They descend through a crevice, toward valleys, taking all morning, and Thurlow's awake now; yet he still feels how slow the day came upon him, and, looking back, sees her walking behind him, freshly, as though sleep's burden was taken, as though he slept her sleep for her, her heaviness pressing him deeper into caves of the mountains, where bears still slept long, all her weight sunk down in his. But he is awake now, obsessed by her. He feels nothing lies before him, but the descent they're making, from high in the mountains, from outcrop to outcrop. They come to a grassy space of rolling vined mounds, where pine boughs fell in storm. They follow a thin animal track. Thurlow wonders what animals came there, why they didn't remain where the day is pleasing. Then he knows what animals passed recently; just ahead, made of boughs and leaves hung upon vines between trees, figures hang jostled, wet laundry heavy on the line, scarecrows meant to be human; five dolls sway and fascinate the traveler, vegetable figures dance in the high wind, guarding an entry to the nearby gorge. Thurlow stares deep into the earth; it opens. He sees a sudden chasm, made by man; he believes he sees a man impaled in the trap, deep on the stakes, and he says, as Marie approaches, they must go another way.

Marie says no, they must . . . But she's also come to the trap, never meant, they believe, for the inhuman beast it caught, never for the ram that fell in, but invented for trespassers, like Thurlow and Marie, for outsiders who come too near. Marie knows these cliffmen don't trust anyone outside. Suddenly she feels removed from those natives. The few she met looked at her with curiosity, as if they were animals wondering what kind she was. She couldn't understand their spoken language, only their rudimentary language of signs, their undeveloped, close gestures; even that wasn't the full sign language she knew.

Now she and Thurlow study the animal shape below them, which must once have been tempted, ridiculously, by those almost human figures swaying between trees, this male goat who came too far from his fear of men, as if he didn't care any more; the goat broke through the disguise, where the pit pretended the earth was safe for the passage of men or animals; some unusual attraction undid him, as if he'd been, like a man, tempted to touch the browning figures, bough and leaf suspended on the vine. Then he writhed on the stakes, dug them into his death; the goat is still. He might have been sacrificed for Marie and Thurlow, to warn them, as the trap's broken surface marks his descent and their danger.

Thurlow says that they'll have to climb around, they aren't wanted.

But Marie says they must go on, that the Indians of the gorge might know of Dutch and Berrigan.

Thurlow says they wouldn't have come here, knowing they weren't wanted, not even Legget.

Marie protests that they may still know something, are even likely to know; but at last she appears to agree with him. Thurlow watches her eyes carefully. Her eyes change. She says she's thankful for his guidance in danger.

Thurlow shrugs and leads the way to a more difficult trail they crossed before, a higher way. Much later, they see, down a thousand feet of rock, the river curled through the gorge.

Thurlow, on the gorge's rim, is frightened by the silence of the pit the ram fell in. Soon it will be dark; he wishes to speak to the woman, wishes her to reply to him, so he won't be alone here. He asks her to tell him about her children and husband. How old are they? What is his name?

Marie tells him, thinking of the valley where Berrigan will descend to their home. She thinks he'll come; he'll remember how he sighed and watched, how he handled the birth of his children. His legs will root in the meadow grass, his head grow huge with painful horns. He'll remember how he held his fingers at the candles, as though to seal and join the little lives of children to the life of the parents; waking briefly, she'd seen him. She'd said his name. Berrigan will come and find Marie asleep in their bed, under piled furs heavy as her sleep; though it will be summer. He'll pile his own sleep's skins in a corner, not to disturb her; he'll take his rest, his pulse slowed in the summer as though winter spread its cold comfort upon them. In Berrigan's dream, a young woman's eyes will enlarge like his head. Her forehead will shine when Marie wakes, after her long sleep. The woman who wakes, Marie or Sawpootway, will stir Berrigan to see the girl Dutchess, and they'll lay hands on a grandchild that has no sex.

Marie remembers her father feeding on rattle-snakes, how he fed her mother and her through long, childhood winters. She remembers how his body came apart and how she replaced his parts with those of a man she killed. After Berrigan took her, she sewed and sewed, as if to recompose and seal her father's body.

A spider web falls across Thurlow's eyes, and he paws, in haste. He wants to see the valley and lake clear when they arrive, water more tempting than figures made by the cliff-dwellers; he's afraid he'll still be blind when the lakes arrive, still retain, too much, the dangling figures above the trap. He says he'll set snares in the valley, for rabbits, and get them meat. He says he'll get the rabbits while Marie catches fish on long, stripped boughs pointed to kill: the boughs will pierce the fish and bend under their weight; from the rabbits, Thurlow will remove the livers, carefully. The lake will soothe them. Perhaps the boy, Dutch, waits there, in some near valley by some near lake. He tells her that; he heard her mumble once that Dutch will be there. Thurlow says it as his voice fades into her silence. She doesn't ever answer him, in that descent; so, though he would now speak more of the rabbits, forgetting her fish, planning his activity, he can no longer speak, as if Marie's silence held him back from words. Thurlow throws his fists up toward a dark figure, probably only a rock, and he shakes them as if to signal someone invisible above the pines; then he covers his reddening face with spread fingers, surprised to find his tears well up.

Thurlow comes to a stop. Marie bumps into him, as he removes his hands from his eyes. Marie moves past him, and thinks Legget shall whip his mule through new, falling snow; each stride shall sink them deeper. Her son shall lie somewhere, hidden under furs. She stumbles, and Thurlow catches her arm, as the air cracks around them in swiftly gathered dark clouds. Thurlow returns in that touch, comes close to her own pursuit of her son. They veer down toward greenness, beneath the Indians they didn't stop to question.

Thurlow says, his voice recovered, that they'll find Dutch now, and he believes what he says. They will find him. He guides her on, and no longer cares where he is or why he's come with her. He shares her faith. He knows they must have meat soon, something bloody, something more animal than snow families, and he's sick of the small, black roots that curl, undissolved, in his stomach, as though they wish to be elsewhere.

At last, she almost speaks one whole sentence to him, saying yes, look at how the . . .

When she speaks, Thurlow thinks he has her now, and doesn't care that her answer falls like the tails of the roots, dropping off through the air into melted snow, leaving small, dark holes where they disappeared. The lake rises, like a mirror Thurlow imagines, and shows the two of them, how they go arm in arm. He's careful not to hold her too close, helping the pale woman down toward the water, careful not to tell her he believes he holds her now, for his own. For the first time since his mule died, Thurlow thinks of his past life, remembers especially how he preached to his congregation like slaves. Now *he* serves Marie, believing service makes her his, aids her down the steep, green incline, beneath the aspen trees.

THURLOW WISHES ONLY TO WATCH HER stoop forever, her body's movement under the leather, the rounded haunches, as she kneels to wash the fish; but since they've come to the lake, he feels that a mystery, alien to him, has entered her like a lover, taken her with the smoother hand. Just when he thought he possessed her, she's possessed by some calming spirit, and she's become indifferent to him. Thurlow feels he can almost see that inimical one, an obscurity almost as palpable to him as her own solid figure. He sees the foreign, new spirit like her shadow on the water. Such near vision, such recognition of the enemy's shape, brings Thurlow a kind of peacefulness of his own, an expectancy and patient surrender to his future; he has learned, from her obsession, how to wait, expecting that spirit's eventual departure, when they find her son or don't find him. Then Thurlow shall move, he believes, from this poised intent at the brink, to enter what he dreams he'll become with her.

When she's cleaned the fish and laid their now lighter bodies on a wide, flat stone, she doesn't leave the water. Marie peers into it, intent on each least ripple of the lake. When she rises, it's only to remove her two garments. Then, from the shore, she returns to the water, she wades in slowly, her body's gradual descent like one of Thurlow's daydreams come true, the wide hips and her walk more solid than the strong morning light that moves on the lake, her heavy breasts, once shared by twins, her dark hair fallen on the lighter skin, all before she swims; then buttocks flash and disappear, and she stands, water to her chin. Head down, she watches again.

Thurlow doesn't think of swimming. He only knows this waiting till she returns, will know another waiting then; for she hasn't looked his way since dawn, seldom seen him in the three days, lingering by this lakeside. Her concentration seems gathered to itself alone, like the concentration of her body in this study of the water, all attention, as if she dived into herself, into the life of her madness, to swim from him. Thurlow tries to remember congregation women he loved without touch. He squats on his heels to try, but finds no past to remember, not even the abyss, behind this time and experience with Marie, that he'd feel if he forgot his past, if he really existed before he met her. He must have done something without her once, and he tries to build, at least, that abyss in memory, of forgetfulness, at least that feeling of loss. He can't. Only mildly disturbed—to his surprise—he squats, pastless, like a young child staring into his preconception, figuring—only in this patience—a future for which this waiting is his preparation.

And it's then she cries out; Thurlow looks up, startled, because he forgot to watch her. Now he too sees, far out, the black figure, a small boat move around a quirk in the valley. Thurlow stands and calls her back, afraid she'll swim to the boat. He saw numerous signs of animal life the three days they've wandered beside the lake, and also signs of Indians' coming and going. He thinks these must be Indians on the lake, canoeing. He remembers she's an Indian too; he still calls her back, to shelter her against her own dangerous desire. She doesn't seem to hear him. She stands still, deep in the water, only her head apparent. Thurlow calls again, never shouting. There's no need to shout and he knows it; he's still too patient to make that mistake. He can't make out figures in the boat, and realizes the boatman or boatmen can't possibly see Marie, her body so hidden by water. But she begins to swim toward him, as if she heard him; so

Thurlow thinks of his own invisibility, for he stands within the shadow of four pines, dark in his black clothes. He's safe from their eyes, but doubts his previous existence, so much so he's compelled to step from his shadow. He goes down to the lake; it spreads in his eyes. When he bends, embarrassed, he sees he's in the watery reflection, his thin features washed against the land—while Marie comes in—and he wonders at his own foolishness, his exposure, to the distant boat, just to see his own features distorted. Yet he won't retreat again into the shadow of the trees, moved by an obsession he can't understand.

The boat, far behind Marie's swimming body, alters in color. At first Thurlow thinks a mirror or a gun on board has caught the morning sunlight, as the lake has, then believes the boat's afire, as if a single flame leapt on the water like a candle. The fire separates, petals of a flower; then all trace of the small, dark boat departs from his eye. The petals remain, moving wings. The fire comes on, the wood consumed, a rose arriving, and Marie nears the shore. He doesn't say anything. She turns, knee-deep in the lake. Thurlow wonders if she's seen the boat and blaze, but he doesn't care about them. He's lost track of all but Marie. He stares. Her wet skin covers heavy bones. She drops down to hide, or to study underwater once more for some sign of life in the lake. Then he says he doesn't understand why a fire would . . . He doesn't complete the thought, has no idea what he'd say if he'd gone on. The sentence gaps, an impatient act intervenes; Thurlow steps into the water, swiftly away from his patience, and spreads his fingers on her breast.

She hits his nose, and his blood spurts; the clear air reddens. Thurlow, surprised, hears his nose snap more than he feels it. His feet slip. He feels the water when his body falls; he hears the sound of his ears slipping under. He loses, not consciousness, but hope, after his impatience flared as inexplicably as fire he didn't understand on the lake. The boat or fire or rose sinks, as Marie's hands reach down for him; for he will not rise of himself, as nothing revives in Thurlow now so cast down. He sees her face peer in, and it seems more beautiful to him, like the face of a living fish, gazing from another medium, but as meaningless as his wife's imaginary face became in snow, while her eyes look like his children, something run away from home. She lifts him; he falls back onto that past she made for him the last few days. He believes that's his only life, before which he wasn't conceived or born, and he can't go beyond this last moment, nor before that first one when he watched her sleeping, and he lingers, as she raises his clumsy body, at the rim of his birth that even she can't move him beyond. Yet Thurlow knows, even in this worst moment, that he must continue to live on in the body she seems to provide. He would dissolve without her, Thurlow disappearing into the forgotten words of an old sermon he preached to his congregation, wishful speech of life beyond the settlements, of settlements in unused lands, language of a mission he felt his own. He wonders if he's even madder than the Indian woman. With difficulty, she tugs his limp body to shore. He knows there's nothing left of his mission: his preaching was taken long ago, by the new land, by the emptiness of plains, now broken in knowledge by the rocks, his mind washed by the lake in which he almost drowned.

MARIE PULLS ON THURLOW'S ARMS, which won't lift themselves, and she pulls his body to shore, with difficulty at first, but once she's moved him he seems light, boneless and puffed with air, floating on the shallow water. Working, she scans the lake for the boat, which won't reappear. She searches for some dark form that would indicate a boy or man swimming or emerging, but she sees no one. She thinks of a plan she conceived, something she yet may do—to slip away from Thurlow and visit the cliff-dwelling tribes. She thinks those people are like her after all. On shore, she pumps Thurlow's shallow chest and flails his arms; she sucks at his breath. He vomits and chokes, then breathes more clearly, his opened eyes deep and surrounded by a new darkness, staring eyes that seem to probe beyond the visible world and her, as if Thurlow looked into his own death, into the death of everything in his own. Marie props him against one of four pine trunks, and she builds up the fire. She has little interest in him any more, and she can't understand why she ever thought he was needed; she wishes he'd disappear now, but his body leans against the tree before her and the fire, and seems to gain solidity as he stares at or through her like a blind man. His body freshens in repose, as if his bones shot new through the pulpy flesh, to strengthen him without her. Yet he doesn't speak, out of that apparent blindness, though she expects him to, and when she turns to walk from the fire, Thurlow doesn't try to follow her, even with his eyes. It is as though he's forgotten her; but she's sad, in the apparent loss of him, only a moment. For the lake is before her, a long clear finger crooked to call her.

She walks, and glances over the smooth surface of the water for a sign of life, of survivors from the wreckage she thought she saw in the distance—a canoe or even a man's hat would do. Now Thurlow's out of sight, and she tells herself he'll be all right. She imagines him under that tree, the steepled pine boughs angled for his shelter. He sits there, in her imagining, like some ill animal a man struggles out of, a man who climbs, like the pine, only to fall again into the old and inhuman form. Then she imagines and tells herself that men will spring from his reclining body like tiny fish; they'll squirm through thin air, their eyes blind, unable to see where they'll fall, invisible eyes obscured by thin blue sheaths as though eyes were knives, and their breath, as if eager from gills, will gasp from their mouths in flight; and all the tiny men will fall like seeds into holes dark in the earth at the base of the pine trees, plunging at Thurlow's still feet, like a spray of needles propelled from the branches above him. She tells herself that Thurlow will glance up swiftly, and rise, dodging aside through the shower of small men from his body, as from green needles or silvery fishfall, and he'll emerge as if he dived through the screen of a waterfall, and he'll plunge to new air as if into the lake, to escape from his own production of risen and fallen men, who're like his own children. Marie shakes, as though Thurlow plunged through her own body. She fears he'll go on alone. She feels very tired: he will come to someone who'll speak to him more than she can speak. He'll move into the eyes of his god, whoever it is, will have childed all over, under the tree, as an animal litters. She's lost hold. He will sit among women, in some later life, like a long, sad hound. Her vision of Thurlow no longer seems her own: he escapes to his future. She believes he'll be beautiful then, like an animal. And he'll no longer try to be human, nor expect a human death. He will grow languorous and old, and he'll put his tongue to the water with love. He will freeze, a paw raised, and will point into trees, like those pines Marie approaches on the lake side. And she's sure, as though Thurlow pointed him out, that she'll find her son on this lake, surviving catastrophe, near drowning. Her eyes and mind betray her, while those trees assume peculiar shapes, becoming various animals before they become just wood again. These transformations of the trees neither worry nor frighten her; but images of Thurlow she hoped to forget are so tiring she must rest for a time. She sinks down in the shadows and shuts her eyes.

AFTER MARIE SLEPT, AFTER HER SEARCH broke with thoughts of Thurlow, after she woke and continued, it is Legget she believes she sees first, damp and huffing on the shore, recovering from the water, sitting under a tree. She's come far, but she doesn't know how far, nor why Legget hasn't yet dried out; the boat sank so long ago. He stares up at her; he makes a sound like snoring, as though he sleeps. She squats and feels for the knife within her blouse. His eyes follow her hand; her hand moves so slowly, as if to treasure its act. He smiles at her suddenly. Then she stops her hand and she asks where Dutch is; she asks Legget what he's done with him.

Legget, in his turn, asks her why she did it, why she played the foolish trick on him. Who did she think he was? Why did Berrigan and Dutch go along with her? When she doesn't answer immediately, he seems to have no more to say, but he points over her shoulder at the lake.

Marie turns her head so she can see the lake and still watch Legget. The shape of water at this point is one she seems to remember from the past, and the trees seem to be trees she saw before: the impression worries her, distorting her purpose, and she wonders what this scene would be if her son, Dutch, came looking for her, not her for him, if he descended to this lake and saw the boat burn, and saw Legget, wet and still pointing as though to deride his hope of finding his mother, Legget like a guardian, pointing toward his mother's death by drowning.

She mutters, asking if he's drowned, and she sees Legget shake his head no, still pointing at the water or at the plateau beyond. Only the slightest ripples disturb the lake; but over the plateau's white snow, clouds roil up darkly.

Marie asks him what he's pointing to, still frightened for her son. When he doesn't answer, she seizes his arm angrily, and pulls it sharply down. She thinks of her knife, again her hand doesn't move. She studies his eyes; for his eyes point too, beyond her face, to something on or over the water, and she can't see what he sees, or what he thinks he sees. She studies his eyes to see what's reflected there: they pierce her, like her son's eyes, but they're red and dark-rimmed as if Legget hasn't slept in a long time. She puts her hand on his shoulder and says to show her. At her touch, his eyes fade to a softer stare; his body relaxes under her gentle grip, as if some purpose goes from him, or a guilt went away, long hidden from others. And he speaks, once more, to say her family must be worried about her, now she's gone so long. He speaks to her strangely, as if *she's* the missing one, as if Dutch and Dutchess and Berrigan wait somewhere for her, missing her, worrying where she could be.

Then, in his eyes, there is Dutch, twice reflected, as sitting beneath a similar tree on the opposite shore. There is Dutch doubled in Legget's eyes, but no Dutch over the lake when she turns. It's as though her son lives only in the membrane, cast by Legget's imagination, invisible outside the soft and staring eyes, eyes as far from her as fish eyes she imagined deep in the lake.

Marie demands that Legget let Dutch come to her. And Legget, as if he's just noticed her, smiles agreeably and rapidly blinks his eyes, as if he'd clear them of Dutch's image. The twin images of her son enlarge like dark pupils and begin to merge, and she remembers me, that I loved her once but learned my love too late, whose son Dutch might be, remembers me as if I am her son, or her son is me, our figures merging; her two sons, reflected in Legget's eyes, join to replace the figure of Legget under the tree, overcoming Legget as her old lover, or young son, descends through her misery, to preserve her life on this lake, to return her, past enemies and obsessions, to a sanity greater than she's known before, a new ease entering her life. This moment of repose won't last, she knows, but when reflected images merge, Legget disappears and, overwhelmed, she forgets me.

There's only Dutch, her son, who says he's looked for her everywhere, and no thing would tell him where to find her. So he said to each animal, each vegetable, and stone if it remembered how his mother brought him this way, to ask protection, and all promised but the green pine needles, who would have nothing else stay green so long; he asked if each remembered who he was. He said the mountains rumbled, the peaks told him how to come to her.

So Marie says she's found him, that they'll go home.

Dutch looks down at the toes of his boots; he frowns and shakes his head slowly. When he looks up again, he sees beyond her, as the fish saw in her previous vision of Dutch beginning to live; Dutch points like Legget.

Marie turns fully about, toward the lake and the plateau, forgetting to keep her watch on the figure of Dutch. A white bolt pierces the piled dark clouds; the lightning strikes through her eyes. Snow, piled on the flat mountain, flames, the white fire, an avalanche flame sliding down, smooth animal smoke, and the lake catches too, like a pool of oil. The colors go wild; shattered rainbows blind her. So Marie thinks she's blind when she turns and can't see him any more.

She sees, instead of her boy, a figure of leaves and mud propped under the tree, holding a needled and coned pine bough between his legs, the long green bough pointing over the lake. Then she weeps, for the second loss of her son, and she covers her eyes, so she can't see he's gone. She rises and stumbles in circles, blindly, till she falls to her knees before the mud and vegetable figure. She drops her hands and stares at the gesture of the bough; she can't conceive, in that moment, that it can mean anything but mockery of her loss.

She imagines Berrigan, lying on his back by a stream, will raise his leg and carefully cut, into his thigh with his knife, as she's seen him open fish to clean them. His blood will run like the lightning to pool. Gently he'll probe his wound, till his fingers extract the tiny son, Dutch, perfect in features and proportions, and, but for size, just as Marie saw him, under the tree, by this lake. She sees the adult child, and she cries; tears change her vision. Now Thurlow kneels beside her, the leaf and mud image gone. He seems to have moved to her from under the tree, or she's walked on to him, circling the whole lake. He brings her up to her feet, to help her home he says. Four white rabbit pelts hang from his belt, and she leans against the white fur, as he speaks of the meat he provided. He thinks she may have no will of her own now.

She says she must go home, to her daughter.

Thurlow imagines that daughter, a smaller replica of the mother. He believes he's found himself again, his future opening from his sleep and rabbit killing, and he leads her homeward; she tells him her son's gone to his father. Berrigan will bring Dutch home, when only Dutchess will be gone. He doesn't ask how she knows these things; she wouldn't be able to tell him.

Marie hangs upon Thurlow's arm, forgetting her son and me, forgetting Legget, her husband LeGuey, others she knew; and forgets the silver knife, in her upper clothes, hidden and cold as a fish between her breasts. She gains strength, but Thurlow still holds her, risen in the hope of making her his, despite his error, his impatience, risen to lead her on into a life of his own, if he can find such a life while he guides her toward home. He didn't expect, when he got to his feet, to find her so malleable, to find her only wanting to go home.

She says she found her son.

Then she can't speak any more, for a long time, absorbed, in interior vision that opens continually, yet is only the reflection, within, of her own face, and her absorption the calmest recognition of her sanity's return. She thinks she doesn't mind being mad, doesn't even desire that calmness descending like a white cloud; for Marie, the acts of madness are only the movements of a god she wouldn't resist if she could. She's sad to see the god departing; leaving madness, she feels blinded, without the ecstasy of the search, in the sober acceptance of features she knows are her own.

DUTCHESS LAY IN HER MOTHER'S BED, covered with a skin. Naked, Adams leaned his elbows on the window sill, sitting by Dutchess while she spoke of her life in the valley. Only his face was dark from the sun; his hands were as pale as his belly. He moved one from his chin, to place it on the deerskin covering her hip; he watched her or he watched the eastern mountain. He could see the pines of the stream, off to his right, but not the cottonwood. He wasn't listening closely. He thought of the fish swimming in the water, and he felt hungry.

The sun rose clear above the twin peaks, in reflections so bright he couldn't watch the peaks any more. He was hungry and he wondered when she would wake to his hunger, when she'd quit speaking of the time when she'd climbed a tree, when her brother had followed. There'd been a small house in the cottonwood tree, one their father built them. When Dutch came near, she'd climbed still higher. She stirred leaves that fell down about him, twigs. He must have thought the twigs and leaves fell from an animal's movements. He must have thought she still slept in the house. Each had climbed to get away from that house, yet to see what their parents did there, things they'd heard the sound of, to watch, through the candlelit window. The children had been very young. From the tree, they couldn't even see as much as they'd seen through the house's interior curtain. Eventually, they'd met in the tree, frightening each other, and neither would admit what foolishness caused their climbing; neither would say if he'd climbed before or seen anything.

Adams listened to a bird call while she talked and became aware of his penis, soft all the time he'd sat there, rising again as if in reply to the bird. He thought he'd slip his fingers, in his silence, into her, to probe her gently; but she struggled and spoke of soreness. He removed his hand, brushing his own thigh, leaving her wetness on him, even a spot of blood on his thigh, and finger. She talked on, as if under a compulsion, not breaking her speech for a moment. He believed she'd be ready for him, when speech had wound itself out, when she'd finished with stories of childhood and trees.

Then he thought he'd like to enter that creek outside, slide in smoothly, let the water sting and cool him. He thought of her brother. The year before he'd camped with four other men, and traded with Berrigan; Dutch had come there. There was a strong resemblance between brother and sister, yet they seemed entirely distinct creatures, of different races, the brother, Adams remembered, in the firelight, as though he were made of an unbreakable glass, unlike his sister's softness in pain and pleasure, as if each were shaped differently from the core, distinguished, one from the other, even more sharply than sex distinguished men and women. The figure of Dutch, standing beside his father, had been frightening, as if he weren't to be moved from some clear purpose, as if it were dangerous to stand in his way.

He heard Dutchess again, talking about that cottonwood and another time, something happening there he didn't understand. He thought he must have missed something, the meaningful part of her tale, and he felt guilty. Her talk continued, how they'd climbed down and sneaked into the house together, the voices of their parents, covering small sounds of entry. Adams looked at her. Her eyes were closed, her body still, only the mouth and tongue moving.

When he looked out the window, he broke into her talk, to say men were coming, three of them. He'd drawn his head back sharply. He found his breeches and began to slip into them. Dutchess raised herself on her elbow, tensed to look out. Three men rode down the valley, down the creek, under the mountain, come down from the pass to the river. They stopped by the stream a half mile away, and began to unsaddle their mounts, their blue guns shiny on the ground in bright sunlight. Two of the men knelt to lap water, while the third brought the animals to drink. Adams said he knew who they were. Dutchess said they were intruders.

Adams said they'd want water only, or to trade for food, or other supplies. He had his breeches on, said he'd see what they wanted.

Dutchess said no, she'd go and speak with them; they'd soon go away.

Adams repeated that he'd go, putting his shirt on as he spoke, adding that it wasn't the kind of business for a girl.

Dutchess laughed; she stood up and let her dress fall over her body. She told him to stay. She said she didn't want them to see him; she was sure they knew her father.

Adams said he didn't have to hide anything from her father; but his face became red. He repeated that he knew them.

She said he must hide for her sake. It was what she wanted.

He wouldn't speak. He saw her go out the door, and she reappeared walking up the creek toward the men. They watched her come. They stood absolutely still beside the water, and waited for her, as if paralyzed by the girl's approach. Adams, though resigned to hiding, grew angrier with them. There were, he thought, probably no other white men, in hundreds of miles, but himself, Berrigan, Legget, and these three men. He didn't count the half-breed, Dutch. Why did these three interrupt now?

When Dutchess got there, they were all so far away that Adams couldn't see their lips move. The necks of the horses arched down to the grass, graceful, bowed. Adams imagined the grass rose through their mouths, mixed with the heavy saliva, up over the long tongues, up the longer necks and down into flat bellies; they were good horses, Adams thought, better than the men who rode them. The mules weren't interesting to him; there was no fineness in them. He closed his eyes, no longer saw the horses, but imagined them.

He seemed to dream, perhaps to sleep, before the window, and he saw himself, or someone who reminded him of himself, stand on a small rise of ground, surrounded by three horses. A creek flows nearby, and it's night, moonlit, for horse teeth like small knives flash from surrounding gums, from jaws. Nearby, the remains of a campfire smolder, the spark preserved in a white mound of ash, like a young girl's cunt. He struggles with the horses on the hillock and prays for help to come in time. He wishes he never left New York, never left the farm.

Adams, still frightened by the dream-fight, opened his eyes and saw two Indians, a man and his squaw, standing across the valley from Dutchess and the hunters. They seemed to have come for water; for they held skin bags; but they hesitated, seeing the white men and the half-breed girl. They moved on down the valley, apparently unobserved by anyone but Adams. He lay back on the bed. He didn't want to watch Dutchess talk to those men.

On the hillock, when Adams saw it again, there's no fighting now. The largest of the horses bends toward the dwindled fire, disturbing the white mound. Then the three horses become three men, friends of Adams. The large man, and the blue man, and the silver man, all come to congratulate him, to bring his woman presents, toys for their future children. Adams opened his eyes and fought the sleep. He felt he should pay more attention to the men and Dutchess.

The hounds had followed her up the valley. The rooster had rounded a corner, to watch the group by the creek. The sleep lay on Adams, and he leaned his forehead on the sill. He thought he'd traveled too hard.

The four men, including Adams, sit on the hillock, warming their palms and fingers and their toes, their insteps at the rebuilt fire, and the one who is most agile—throughout his body, like a fish—speaks, while the one with horned hat and the one like a fox nod their heads in agreement or in near sleep; the agile one says that once they came to this valley, out of the lower earth, and the mountain refused them. Then they descended like worms, when the white horns turned red like the flames of candles, to the land they came from. He says that Adams, with the Indians' help, destroyed them, and a man on a mule pursued.

Adams says no, that he was hidden from them, that his wife only went to them, because he feared her father. He says he spied on them from a window in his house, sitting on his own bed while an Indian and his woman passed, to gather water farther down the creek, Indians the three men didn't even see go by. Adams says the Indians didn't help him.

The large man, with the buffalo hat, asks where Marie is. He hoped to see her with Adams.

Now Adams knows they confuse him with somebody else, with Berrigan. He says he doesn't know where she is. He says his name is Adams, not Berrigan. He looks about for Dutchess, to identify him, and he realizes she wasn't and isn't there.

The large man asks if he's missed Marie this time too. He places his hands over his eyes.

The three men sit in silence, sadly, holding forth their hands, before Adams, leaping up above the warming flames, asks them where Dutchess is, where she went. All the men stand, and revolve in place, as if they turn in fire, while Adams, the horses and mules, stare at them.

Adams used his fingers to help open his eyes; and Dutchess, present in daylight, not lost after all, had turned from the three men. The sleep left him. The rooster went out to meet her; but Adams waited in the room; his body relaxed. He realized his dream hadn't been set in this valley, but in some other, far away, in another kind of country; and knew that the fish-like man had spoken, in dream, as if they were under this twin-peaked mountain when they weren't.

Adams, for a moment, resented that deception, and the way they'd confused him with Berrigan. The hounds stopped outside with the rooster; Adams didn't like the dogs coming with her, to him, into the house.

Her first words were meant to reassure him. At the creek the men were eating the dried meat they carried. Dutchess said they'd wanted nothing but water, but they might return, after some hunting. She came to Adams, and knelt on the floor. She undid his breeches; she held him fast, in wonder that he swelled in her fist. He raised her up to the bed. She said they'd seen her mother, that they'd seen her looking for Dutch. Her mother had said Legget stole Dutch. They thought it was funny.

Adams didn't smile; it wasn't funny to her. He said they would elope, that he and she must; for this was not the place to live. He felt the dream had spoken through his mouth.

She laughed, because what he said surprised her. She asked where they would go.

He said that, for now, they'd go to a place where two rivers joined, where a city was growing, across the plains and prairies. Those men believed she was alone.

She said they wouldn't go, quite yet. They lay down together, though Adams was nervous about the men eating at the creek. Dutchess said yes, it would be good to elope, almost as if he came and stole her; but they wouldn't yet; there was her father and mother, her brother to think of. She laughed, and he looked at her face, confused by her changes. She said if they did go, they wouldn't be there when the others came home.

Adams also laughed. He said they could leave word

for the others, on a piece of wood.

She said they wouldn't leave pictures of animals though.

Adams said no, just their names on the bark of that cottonwood tree she talked so much of, or pictures of them as they were now, or as they'd soon be.

By morning, Adams had almost persuaded her, and had made their plans. They'd leave a message, on paper, fastened to the parents' bed.

AT EVENING, WHILE HE CLEANSED HIS feet in the stream, Orcus Berrigan sat naked on the white stone, dead fish fanned out beside him. The late sun rimmed the nearest heights; beams, long and angular, bent upon the water, the white rock, his knife, the dead and fading bodies of the fish. Berrigan's nakedness was whiter than the rock's white; only his hands were dark and his head, as if three things weren't part of his real body, head and two hands stuck on in afterthought. Dark fingers probed between pale toes; his dark, shaggy head bent watching.

He heard a meadowlark call and another one answer, then another bird call, and another answer. On the third repetition of that bird dialogue, Berrigan released his toes and raised his head to listen more intently; he placed his palms firmly on the rock; he extended his toes and calves into the river. The repetitive game of song continued, while Berrigan cocked his head to the brief phrases, each phrase identical, like the mark of the voice, its signature.

Berrigan felt his cock stir, irrelevantly, without

stimulus, the hard growth against his thigh. He moved one hand as though to hush that unwilled motion. Accidentally he felt the dead fish he'd forgotten. That memory made him shrink, and he raised his knife, to clean fish again. He gutted the first one with ease, in silence; then, as he cut through the belly of the second, the bird, after a pause, called again, again was answered. Berrigan's knife slipped, and sliced his thigh instead of the fish. The cut was shallow, only a thin line of blood formed under his pressing fingers, the red line so clean in the banks of skin, while the bird calls continued and changed. Berrigan peered into the wound; his fingers spread skin to increase his bleeding, made a tiny pool of blood in the furrow of his thigh.

Now no first bird voice called, but the one that had answered, distinguished by lower tones, played on both parts, as though the other bird had been consumed in his single voice. The sound approached through the trees, and Berrigan, suddenly apprehensive, slid from his stone into the water, as if he'd hide from the bird's voice; the water stung him with sudden cold, as he peered around the rock toward that song.

A man came, out of lodge-pole pines, toward Berrigan, who, startled, slunk lower beneath the rock before he recognized his son. Dutch walked, whistling, aware of no one. Berrigan stood and rose toward the shore.

Dutch stopped sharply, both his walking and bird tune. He stared at his naked father, who surprised him, in coincidence on this shore, so far from the valley. And he flinched slightly, when Berrigan trotted toward him unashamed; he saw his father's balls swing heavily, the cock fly about, these ridiculous things in the scene of greeting, and he saw the red line the knife had cut in the thigh. Orcus Berrigan came and spread his arms.

Dutch stood straight and tense in his father's embrace, his own hands placed lightly on the other's sides, then he stepped back, shoving his father lightly, against the belly and chest, with loosely closed fists. For a moment they stared at each other, the father strained forward in his eagerness of greeting, the son wary like an animal, before Berrigan said, "Welcome back, Dutch," and Dutch nodded, knowing something had changed for good. What was said sounded silly to him; the sound of his father's voice was even more startling than his presence in this place, more startling than his nakedness and embrace; it didn't seem to Dutch that any human being could possibly have spoken here, though he'd heard Legget's voice only recently. He couldn't speak; he felt he'd forgotten how to speak to his father. He was ashamed.

Berrigan turned toward the stone, and Dutch walked by him until he saw the fish. He strode forward more quickly than his father could easily move, bare feet too tender on the stones. Dutch seized the knife, to work, avoiding speech.

Berrigan dressed slowly, like a lover reluctant to leave the bed where a woman sleeps. He studied his son, grinning as if he understood that eagerness for cutting fish. He asked, "Where's Legget?"

Dutch shrugged, and stooped to the water with an opened fish, the light interior flashing down, the trout spread by his thumbs.

"Can't you answer?" Berrigan asked. He pointed, "Can't you say more than those fish?"

Words trickled from Dutch's mouth, like the water from lifted fish. "I don't know," he said.

"What happened?"

"He let me go. I left him." His own voice sounded unfamiliar to him, shocking, as if it belonged to another and shouldn't have sounded in the humid air.

"Why?"

Dutch shrugged; he didn't speak. He straightened up and turned toward his father, as if to ask *him* why.

Berrigan said, "What did he say to you?"

"Nothing. Just let me go. Nothing else. And I came away from him."

Berrigan asked, "How did he take you?"

Dutch continued his work. "He hit me with the rifle barrel. When I woke, I was tied on that mule's back." In his left hand he held a fish, in his right the knife; both hands became still. He glanced over his shoulder and said, "Smoke, its name is," as though the mule's name were the most important thing he had to tell.

"Smoke." Berrigan shook his head slowly, while Dutch turned his face away.

"I was scared when I woke up."

"Yes."

Now Dutch seemed to have broken through; now speech came easy, as if his voice had thawed out. "But I was more scared when he just let me go, when he didn't say anything else, not what for, but just untied me from a tree I'd been leaning on, sitting there looking up through the branches, through the needles, and I was sort of daydreaming, of that treehouse we used to have in the cottonwood, and sort of daydreaming about what I'd do if I was him, when he just let me go, and I stood up, kind of stiff and scared, and looked at him while I brushed myself off, the needles from my butt, and he moved his hand in front of his face just once, like this, like he was brushing the sight of *me* off of him; then he turned away and he walked back to where he sat before, by the fire, and he sat there again, and he put his elbows on his knees and covered up his ears with his palms like this, like he just didn't want to hear me, though I didn't say a thing, with his eyes tight closed too, like he wouldn't see me go."

"So you came away."

Dutch seemed out of breath: "Yes. I saw your fire and smoke."

When he'd finished dressing, Berrigan stood silent for a time, behind his son, staring, as though absorbed in himself, as if Dutch didn't really exist for him any more; then, as if he surprised himself, he asked, "And what would you have done, if you'd been him?"

Dutch was finishing the last of the fish. Berrigan asked again. "Released me," Dutch said, spreading that trout. "What good was I to him? Released me."

AT THE MOMENT BEFORE DAWN, THEY departed together toward home. They anticipated the light that rose soon at their backs, casting their shadows ahead. Then the shadows of father and son stood upon the steep mountain to greet them, an intimate darkness, as though they'd enter shadows like new selves: at least something, if not the sun, eased them early in that morning, at least something, if not the shadows drawing the two men, urged them to ascend the hard slope of the mountain Berrigan called Eagle's Beak. The peak above gestured like a finger, or like the closed, raised beak of the bird of its name. To move beyond, they had to climb up to the pass a hundred yards below the beak or finger, and they made the pass by noon, to sit, within the rock walls, without any shadows, as though their bodies had consumed, ascending, the darkness bodies cast that morning. They ate of the fish, brought from below.

Berrigan leaned on his gun, as he ate, while Dutch squatted and asked, "Why do we do what Mother says?"

"We don't," Berrigan said. "We don't always."

"We do. We did that trick. And it was foolish and no reason for it," he stared down at the fish in his hands.

"That man, Legget, might have done something to Dutchess. Your mother might have been right." Berrigan spoke to the distance, to the peak or the sun, and he didn't believe what he said.

Dutch said, "He did do something."

Berrigan didn't want to talk about it. "I mean something worse," he said; but he didn't know what.

Fish eaten, Dutch said, "No. That's only what Mother feared, what she told me before I went down. That's what she said, and she's . . ."

Berrigan wiped his sweat, and he said, his anger evident, "No, I was against it. It won't do to say I wasn't." Dutch said nothing. Defensively, Berrigan said, "You know I was."

Dutch did look up then, unsmiling. "So if there's blame to lay, it's on my head?"

Berrigan laughed. He said, "Come on."

They moved into the pass, past the thick, dark rocks, snow streaks like markings of a bird. Dutch said, "Least of all you wanted it, for him to take her away. So whatever reasons Mother had, even if she is . . . She was right in the end." They continued, side by side, northwest through the pass; the shadow grew upon them. Then the son stopped, so Berrigan turned toward him. Dutch asked, "You think he'll try again? Does it mean he's given her up, that he let me go like that?"

When Berrigan shrugged, his whole body moved, as though he'd shed water. In the shadow of afternoon, his son's eyes pierced more than the obstructed light, concentrated like diamonds in dark holes, caves of sleep he lacked. His father took him by the shoulder. Again he said, "Come on." He said, "Your mother and sister are alone."

Dutch's eyes faded to staring, into dullness, a different focus, as if into the guilt he'd spoken of, as if he couldn't see Berrigan any more, saw something else or nothing. His body, once so hard in his father's grip, gave up control, as though his will dissolved.

Dutch said, "There are some things I wish I'd done."

"Look, we're going home. We've got folks waiting." With great effort, Dutch recomposed himself. "Yes, they must be worried about us now." He walked, a little distant from his father, and Berrigan was careful not to touch his son, though he wished to bear him home in his arms. He didn't want his son to take so much blame on himself, the guilt of the abduction. He kept to just the distance Dutch kept between them.

THEY SLEPT ABOVE THE INVISIBLE, GES-turing lake Marie had passed; the white dome of the plateau rose beneath them. Dutch woke before dawn and stood in silence. Eyes on his father, he slipped from their bare camp. He only wanted to be alone for a time, to wonder what had happened. His mind was worried with the trapper, Legget, who still held him, by tenuous, sticky threads. Had Legget, freeing him, been as hopeless as he seemed? He almost wished they'd compelled his sister to go with Legget, to finish the business once and for all time.

Under lowered lids, Berrigan had watched and let Dutch go from the camp, then rose to follow, to see what his son would do, without his interference. Soon, he'd watch Dutch stand still, doing nothing, or so he thought, and he'd call out to his son, at the mouth of a small box canyon.

Dutch moved on the mountainside, with brief views of the snowy plateau, thinking of nothing he knew he was thinking, only letting the thought of his release from Legget turn in him; as though he was indifferent to that thought, which floated like a speck in the corner of an eye. When he wondered, after walking so long in the darkness, what Legget would do, he didn't try to find the answer.

Dutch came, in the first pale light, to a rock-enclosed box, a small canyon through which he could see no further passage; he stopped there, and peered long into its darkness, while the dawn came upon him. Slowly, on a ledge at the far end, a figure took shape, a two-headed creature that, as if shrinking in fear, became part of the wall. Then, in the increasing light, the figure emerged from the darkness; Dutch saw the squat, huddled figures of the man and woman, and he was afraid. They watched him, he realized, as he watched them. Then he made out the child the woman held against her body and the bow the man held, partially concealed, at his side. They didn't move, as if they waited to see what Dutch would do.

The figure of the Indian family held Dutch's vision, as if Dutch couldn't possibly see anything else.

He felt stuck in that one focus, permanently distorted by their image. A stair emerged above them, tiny hand-carved niches of possible escape, part of their image now. Dutch and the Indians stared—Dutch unarmed, and armed Indians—gazed as animals do; they wouldn't approach to inspect each other. Dutch thought again of Legget, a sharp figure rising from dream, as if the Indians had recalled the trapper. Dutch felt Legget had drowned, accidentally, then risen, after an explosion the Indians caused. Dutch released the figure of Legget, shot up in fragments, like successive rifle balls spun through the air, so rapidly they seemed elongated and tailed, balls falling like seed into dark holes like the sockets of Dutch's skull. The bullets grew so long, rapid in air, they seemed, after all, green pine needles or sharp bones spinning, and Dutch felt penetrated, wounded, by Legget's imaginary flight through air, and by the fall down holes like empty eyes; so it seemed that he himself had died and lain, encaved behind a waterfall, that Legget released him from that death Dutch might dive from in escape, pierce the falling screen of water, and plunge into a long lake like a smile, where he saw his mother's body, in imagination, as he'd seen it often, naked, crouched in the creek, washing the few clothes they had that were made of cloth, usually much-rotted clothes Berrigan had brought from Santa Fe, cloth falling more each day from his mother's body. Now he saw her in the body of the water, as though in search, peering down. At some times more than others she'd seemed to prefer the cloth to the leather, cotton to skins, but all cloth fell from her in time. Now her body faded into the waters as though into new clothes; she went into that darkness.

Dutch heard one voice speak, and he answered

without thought, replying to a voice as he had recently to the bird, this time with one word, one question. He asked, "Yes?" He meant to ask who was there. That time before, the bird had disappeared, entered silence, tiring of their game, and he'd said the bird's part of it, whistling brief, repetitive phrases back and forth, as if he communicated with his own voice. Dutch didn't see the Indians any more, that family calling up images, of Legget and his mother. He'd come from his father in the camp, into this morning light as though from a dark cave; now he turned, for the voice had called from behind him, saying something he didn't remember; he remembered nothing but the sound of the voice. He recognized his father. He wondered if Berrigan had seen the Indians, and he glanced into the canyon, only to see that the family was truly gone. As his father came up, Dutch stared into the light that came to that box, and wondered if the figure, the family he'd seen emerge, had been actual.

Berrigan came on, watching his son carefully, in awe, for his son seemed beautiful to him, in the early dawn, so still and steady, gleaming and finely drawn, inpenetrable, unbending.

All day Berrigan would be aware of some change in his son, a look of pleased surprise in Dutch's eyes, renewed confidence in his body. Together they would descend to a lake and would kneel to the water, cupping their hands, licking, sucking the moisture from their palms. Berrigan would glance sideways, continually, at Dutch, who'd seem to him something almost inhuman, like a fish or a god, strange as the animal gods of his wife's tribe. Dutch would then stand quickly from the water, and he'd point into the trees where a doe would pass briefly.

All that day, Dutch would take a new interest in his father, as if he'd just discovered him.

IT WAS MORNING ON THE LAKE. DUTCH swam, his calm, indifferent body in the water, as though the lake was as familiar to him as his skin, his father, watching from the shore, a relative stranger.

Berrigan had seen the young man's white body enter the water, the gathering unloosed; and he remembered me, how he'd loved me before Sawpootway's body opened to him. He remembered how he'd watched from the ravine, above a shore. He'd eaten those berries, that honey, from the rocky place on Corn Island; he'd seen me work my trades of wood and metal, preparing for war, my red hair like a signal. The troopers had gathered in 1779; it was June or July, twenty-one years before. Berrigan had grown less lonely, relaxing more, watched me as a lover might a bathing woman; he'd returned in the ravine to some old feelings about himself, as if into a previous existence he'd forgotten, while the movement of troops, the life on the island in the Ohio, passed over him like water, pierced by his own almost animal indifference. The Dutch I was then mattered to him that moment: he'd cared about the fine berries in his stomach, that stolen honey, and those elements I worked, of wood and metal, if not the very guns, so did the distance matter between us, between ravine and shore. He hadn't announced himself, remained invisible, and chewed the waxy comb.

Now, as he crouched at the fire, cooking for them, his tongue felt huge and thundering in silence against his teeth and palate, as if he had words to say to his son. He thought of Sawpootway, and couldn't remember exactly when he'd first entered the woman; but her parts had burst, opening to him, and he knew images of pink buds or dark fig-centers under his tongue; like a young green bud she revealed new inner layers that stuck more and more to him, the deeper he went. He'd liked each place in her.

That had been his past, me then the woman: she'd entered his life; he watched his son swimming, while he cooked, and he felt he couldn't be right in himself without her, not if they were parted long, as in death; though he knew he'd done something without her once, like seeing me from that island ravine, while honey he'd eaten held small berries to his beard. It didn't seem possible now to do anything without the sense of her presence and participation. Her presence entered even the ravine where he first saw me, before he knew her.

Berrigan cooked the fish, and he wondered, after thoughts of his past, about his future, imagining, peculiarly he thought, a boat, a canoe, sailed into his future, a buckled sheet of red, like blood flared into the wind above the vehicle. He saw Dutch swimming in, and walked down to meet him, thinking of the canoe, thinking it might have sailed without him, disappearing, so only the flames remained on the horizon, till doused, rose petals sinking, then nothing, Berrigan's love of his life blasted so far from him. But he saw his son swimming, and felt, after all, his own presence in his future, sensed in his body the continuance of himself, and he only feared for Dutch's safe arrival on the shore. He knew the fear was silly, and remembered how Dutch had cleaned fish, as if they were part of his own body. He remembered, in the small harbor of Corn Island, he'd floated so securely, himself, while he watched me arrive in a boat. His fear for Dutch departed.

Dutch came safely in the shallow water, unstumbling; he looked back at the lake's long, curved gesture, as if he expected to see something he left behind. The lake was empty, as if what Dutch looked for had gone down the horizon like Berrigan's imaginary boat. Berrigan stepped to a wide damp stone, and extended his hand to his son. Dutch needed no help, but he gave his own hand before, taking thought, he tried to withdraw it. Unbalanced, Berrigan almost fell; he felt as if he sprawled and nearly drowned in humiliation, while the blood roared in his head, like water closing over his ears. He imagined he lay under water, Dutch peering in, searching, concerned, reaching down for him, the son's hand extended again, with a difference. But Berrigan would rise without much help, wet clothes adhering like new flesh. Then his son's eyes would no longer be so alien and beautiful, like the indifferent eyes of a fish or god: all that repose, as though of supporting water, gone, the eyes would leak tears, or be still wet from the swim, like the body.

Berrigan didn't fall. Dutch's eyes, small images of his flesh, seemed Berrigan's own physical future, the only one he could know, as if Dutch had replaced the imaginary boat as the vehicle of that future. Berrigan was glad of the recognition, couldn't understand why it had never struck him so clearly. But with that insight came the small doubt, more piercing than ever —of the son's origin, Dutch's paternity—like a needle into an unfinished fabric, as if into the flesh of an animal that had surrendered its life to Berrigan.

Dutch asked, "Are you all right?"

"Hungry," Berrigan said. He felt guilty for his doubt. He shivered, as though he wore wet clothes.

THE NEXT DAY, A LANDSLIDE, ROCKS previously fallen, forced them to climb from the expected route. Berrigan rose unreleased from his dream of the night, and they returned to the winter. He'd dreamed he slept in the icy, domed plateau. In this morning he moved like a bear who'd come, prematurely, from his cave, his breathing still too slow after the dark sleep. He leaned forward toward Sawpootway and his homecoming; but invisible strands of the landscape below restrained him. They made small progress home. They moved out of the thaw that continued below them. Berrigan wished something would urge him, the spring life rise to his mouth so he'd cry some startling news; he thought what that sleep had been within him, how he'd dreamed he might stay locked in the old ice, his own son locked in his body, his beard growing hoary with the cold of a sleep, his breath too slow for waking, or cracking any ice that both held and preserved him.

At first they didn't speak. Berrigan walked on, Dutch following, through crisp air, fragile like a glass in which Berrigan could see Dutch, the young face thrust forward; he felt they moved into their reflected bodies, their shadows fallen away, into the thaw. He felt they'd vanish into some old story of themselves, where they were speechless, where only another could speak for them. He knew he wasn't yet awake; he journeyed in that dream, in previous sleep.

When Berrigan looked back and down, past Dutch, snow swirled upon the plateau, stirred by wind demons, snow forms like animals and children, strange women and men, familiar yet not quite recognized, like clouds wind shaped above; he knew the plateau's turmoil, the images, in the dim, reflected light, as though in the mirror, the glass of air, as if another life, one that was alien, roiled about the climbers.

They saw animal tracks on the slope, and once, Berrigan imagined, through a screen of snow, he saw Indians with bows at their sides like linked arms, blocking their path, but those natives became, on approach, a few scraggly small pine trees trying to grow too far up the slope, stunted trunks, boughs, branches, a few green needles and tiny brown cones. They did pass a tall burial mound, covered with still green boughs men had brought from below, graves that Berrigan pointed out to Dutch. Then, to break the silence which seemed so integral to cold and sleepiness and to the past dream, Berrigan, falling back beside Dutch, asked if his mother had ever told him who he and Dutchess were named for.

Dutch said he knew the man was a friend.

Berrigan said yes, he was a friend of both of them; but had Dutch ever been told his true name?

Dutch said he knew the name was Gerhard Blau, that his mother had called him, also, the names in her tongue which meant He-for-whom-we-seek-life and Fish-out-of-water, that she spoke of him as though he were one of those gods of her tribe she'd told him about.

Berrigan laughed and said yes, there was that; then he said no, Blau'd been a man like them, no older than Dutch was now.

Dutch asked what happened to him.

Berrigan said the woman, his mother, had told him all this.

But Berrigan hadn't told him, had he?

Berrigan looked away. He said Gerhard Blau might have gone on to Santa Fe; that's where they'd meant to take the gold.

Had Blau helped steal the gold from the British?

No, Berrigan was with Blau afterwards, not then. What had his mother told him?

Dutch wanted to know from Berrigan. His mother hadn't been there either, when they'd taken the gold.

Berrigan asked if Dutch really wanted to know where the gold was. For all he knew, Blau'd taken it all from the Indian camp, after they'd gone; though they'd taken the wagon into mountains.

Dutch didn't want to know about the gold, but had Berrigan never cared what became of his friend?

He'd cared. He'd looked for him in Santa Fe once, without luck. Blau had disappeared from their lives, or they had from his; he'd got to be something, like the gold, they'd lost along the way, something they didn't seem to need any more. Berrigan said they'd felt the loss, and the names of children came of that, for something gone out of life.

Neither man seemed to know what to say then. Dutch felt vague, as if he'd never been fully formed; as in the tale told of bears: that the father must lick to shape the small lump from the female grizzly's belly. There was some question he couldn't quite pronounce to get the answer he needed. He had to ask his father, almost at random, questions he knew answers to already. There was, he asked, someone named Pawkittew, a priest?

Berrigan said yes, there was the ass-priest of the tribe. He spoke as if he were reciting a familiar legend. He said that Pawkittew was a half-breed, a good man who'd helped them come to this country, who'd been translator and guide to the troopers of the Illinois. Called Drake then, he'd become the friend of Berrigan and Gerhard Blau, had followed them when they'd gone from the expedition for the gold, and revealed himself in time to save Berrigan's life from the knives of two troopers and the mother's husband. Then Berrigan fell silent for a time, before he said he wished they'd speak of something else.

Dutch asked what he meant.

He said he meant to keep them warm, to think of home. He would tell Dutch how he imagined it would be when they'd arrive, what he saw then. He didn't tell Dutch he felt he must say something, anything, to change their subject, that he was tired of the recitation of known things. Then Berrigan spoke the longest speech he thought he'd ever spoken at one time, as if his continuing voice could drive the cold and past time from them, as if what he pretended could answer all questions. He was still sleepy, still spoke as though from a dream.

He spoke of the future, saying the valley would seem empty at first, but they'd learn it held Dutch's mother and sister, and hounds who'd greet them, chickens and goats, the horses, the single mule. They'd be glad to get home. As he spoke, Berrigan knew he was weary; he felt his legs would take root in the slope and his head grow huge and painful with something like a dream he woke from. He said their cabin would probably be dark when they got there. Berrigan could see, though he didn't say it, that Dutch would wait outside with the hounds, as if he were frightened to enter with his father. Berrigan would enter and light candles that had burned down to stubs, tallow at their bases too hard to take an impression. The room would feel strange to him, as if the tallow, against expectations, had flowed back into the animals it came from. He no longer spoke to his son. He would find Dutch's mother sleeping under furs; he'd uncover and wake her. He'd see Dutchess, when Dutch finally entered. She'd stand near the door. The eyes of his daughter would enlarge when she saw them, and she'd start with pleasure or guilt; her forehead would shine with sweat in the candle-light. Sawpootway and he would put their hands on the heads of their children, and would speak of grand-children, planning them, and they wouldn't be afraid for others to love their children.

All would sit down at the table, and Sawpootway would speak to the children of their grandfather, Snakesnorter, who'd been a witch of a man; she'd tell how he fed her mother and her with the rattlesnakes who were his intimates, when they'd survived the hard winters of blizzards on the plains, and how he'd died violently, his body torn. She'd tell them how, while Berrigan lay ill, as if dying, she'd restored her father's body, while Gerhard Blau had tried to help her.

They would hear much that Berrigan had always thought they shouldn't hear so young, and they'd al-ways be too young. Sawpootway would sit at the table and stitch, as she told how she'd sewed up their grandfather, shutting him up for the longest winter, when he'd sleep like the bears who'd given him power when he was young. The stories would be like stories for children who never existed, for no one could be the right age to hear them.

The web of these images spread over Berrigan's eyes, a film, a fabric, as he climbed toward the ridge with Dutch. He brushed them away as best he could.

He realized he'd been speaking aloud the part

about Snakesnorter, but had stopped talking then, as if his voice dropped over a precipice, over the ridge before them, and disappeared as if it hadn't ever been heard.

Dutch listened for his father to talk again, but there wouldn't be more till later. He didn't wish to say he'd heard about his grandfather and more, from his mother, or something like it, as if it were a story and stories his mother and father had rehearsed together, though their lines were imperfectly known and no prompter existed to remind them of exact words. He wished, for this moment, to hear his father's voice continuing in his ear; he'd cup it there, in an embrace. And he wanted to hear, without asking for it—he was embarrassed—the story of Berrigan's parents, those grandparents no one ever spoke about. They struggled forward; they passed the ridge.

In the afternoon, they descended and the cold broke from them, disappeared like Berrigan's story, as if it had never held them. They saw western valleys clear before them; Berrigan shot two rabbits, and they stabbed four fish in a shallow stream. They cooked on the stripped boughs they killed the fish with, the flesh and fish spitted over the fire, those animals turning out of life, consumed by two men.

Dutch ate and remembered his father cleaning the rabbits, their livers under his careful thumbs; he remembered how the fish smelled and the rabbits, and he believed they *were* different kinds of animals, as different as gods from men. Berrigans, father and son, ate of both kinds, and Dutch thought how both kinds became one in their bodies. It wasn't yet dark, and he saw a ram above them, the two horns tightly coiled, the male peering down his nose. Amused by that goatly look, he waved up the rock to greet the animal.

That night, as he passed into sleep, he couldn't remember ever having dreamed, but believed he would
dream now; in the past he'd never given room in himself, hospitality, for dreams to enter. He looked at his
father, who appeared to be weeping or troubled by the
smoke from the fire—for the wind had shifted. He
roused himself to ask, to mutter something about his
father's parents, "Died, did they? Your people?" He
knew that wasn't the question he needed to ask; the
real question, he felt, evaded him, running before,
into the dream he'd have. He barely heard Berrigan's
answer.

"No, I think they're alive."

Berrigan wiped his eyes; he felt he must understand something of his son, before they got home. He
answered that his father was a Pennsylvania farmer, an
Irishman who'd sided with the British, his mother's
people; pneumonia took his mother; and "I left
home." That was all he wished to say.

Dutch sank on into sleep with a feeling of danger,
perhaps from what his father said, like a knife poised
to stab, a needle to pierce cloth or leather, tear
through his consciousness; the approaching dream
then seemed the dangerous thing. He thought of
Legget, imagined him alive and riding his mule
through deep snow in the darkness, beneath bright
stars like snowflakes glittering, hung up high. With
each stride the mule hooves stroked deeper, as Dutch
neared his sleep. There were no furs on the mule at
all, and where was Legget going, in Dutch's partial
dream? He remembered that some small, dark roots
he'd nibbled on that morning had tasted good, had
curled in pieces down his throat, seeking their rightful
place inside him. His own valley rose toward him,
like something soon to change, and he didn't see what

it would turn to, risen in such dream, as if from water.

He felt that if he and his father were ever in danger, they were not ever in great danger, despite his sleepy fears, and they'd arrive home, while the valley rose and turned in his dream like a fish; it changed its meaning to something he couldn't quite understand. They would arrive home now, father and son, as though into stories he'd heard before from his mother's lips, yet never before today in his father's voice, which, in memory, seemed like the night fire's warmth. He heard that voice, in the semblance of that pleasant fire, say, "Sleep . . . long way to go yet."

IT WASN'T YET MORNING IN THE MOUN-tains, not yet the light out of darkness, nor the green revealed rising from white winter, nor the white bones exposed like new life in the caves, not all the spring flesh run elusive as fish down the river; but Berrigan rose, groggily, and was limned in the low firelight, before that small, leaping premonition of dawn, a bud of fire so clear in darkness like winter upon him. After finding Dutch, he'd turned from those interior plains east of the mountains, from flat land the sky adhered to like a skin, where he'd left me, years ago, and disappeared toward these mountains with the woman. He thought he would never return again, to plains, not in this single lifetime, in his present body; only Dutch or Dutchess could go there now. He remembered how they'd come to Sawpootway's tribe, on the same river that flowed near their present home.

He remembered I'd been the first one, the first Dutch, on horseback, entering an isolated cottonwood grove, four women with me. There, the Indians would insist one woman conceived a child by me. The future child was why Pawkittew, the half-breed, the ass-priest, had brought me to the tribe, for the conception and growth of a future priest, the half-breed's successor. Berrigan remembered my entry, his old friend's, into that wood, remembered the baffled look on his face; but now it was the figure of his son he saw when he remembered. He wondered, what if his son went there? Would Dutch, arriving, find a young man of his own age, my son surviving? Would he find Pawkittew, the man who'd guided his parents once?

No, Berrigan could see it all, as clearly as though he did go in his present life and body, could see the scene of early summer on that sandy river. Pawkittew, an old man now, would be gone into that exile he must enter when the young man came of age; his absence was the definite, the clarifying element in the scene; and, scarcely less clearly, he saw that the young man, come of age, would be gone also, on a confused mission, with little belief in success, departed to find (the young man would not know which) either another white man, as Pawkittew once sought someone like me, or Pawkittew (who'd gone when the young man thought he needed him most), or me, perhaps his own father (who'd gone maybe toward Santa Fe, leaving the pile of gold). Berrigan couldn't tell why he felt so sure of those things; it was as though he was present, returning after all, or would be.

Berrigan's mind, confused in memory and imagination, twisted and sighed, stranded; Berrigan made the comparison of mind to fish, then suddenly thought and almost said aloud to Dutch that fish were signs of their souls. Berrigan didn't know what that meant and he blushed at the thought of saying what he'd thought about; those sudden ideas, popping like jack rabbits out of holes, were embarrassing, ridiculous, not to be considered beyond their brief appearance. So he thought how they'd eaten fish, thought what he and Dutch would eat this morning: salad of tiny blue berries, brown vines, leaves dark and purple.

And thoughts of the food they ate made him wonder at Dutch's survival, how he'd come, through Legget, to return home with his father. It didn't quite make sense, to vanish so, stolen away, then so easily escape death. But it happened, and who was Berrigan to question what occurred beyond his control? He felt vaguely guilty, for it seemed to him proper that Legget's revenge should succeed more than it had. Could there have been such a survival of his son without the father, without him, if he hadn't come to find Dutch?

The notion was stranger to Berrigan than ideas he'd had of fish, and related notions came. Had Dutch disappeared, when captured, into another life and time? Berrigan tried to understand what he meant, and found, to his surprise, that he wondered if Dutch could exist without him. He wondered if this time, of returning with his father, this existence Berrigan had in mind, seemed quite real to Dutch after adventures of capture and absence. Was Dutch awake now, watching his father above him, or did he sleep, lying so quietly before the dawn, beyond the flames?

Berrigan, who knew all along that he wasn't awake, thought of the river that flowed near his home and now near them, water he'd often drunk from, water that seemed to run deep within him, rising and sinking like Sawpootway's belly more than twenty years ago; her whole body was, to Berrigan, an image of their life together, the falling and return. He remembered her breasts moved, as though from her heart's pulse flushed through her body, beneath the skin, how his own blood was so near hers in their embrace, how it seemed they'd break the skin's restraint, so near each other they knew they were separate creatures, in ecstasy's moment, never to know one another otherwise, unless each beat free eventually in death, pulsed outward without return, into some inhuman afterlife: he didn't desire that death, that inhuman union.

Dutch did lie, awakening, and saw his father; still felt, in sleep, a dream of Berrigan's hair fallen thickly, felt the fullness of his father's hair, as the dawn seemed near; hair must seem so heavy to his father, so severe, impressed into skin and skull. Could his father lose it all, become bald, that hair fall out like long, soft, pine needles to dry and curl hard? Or could hair, like his dream, furl and fold outward, fly up, turning to birds or fish, developing, in a new complexity, a message Dutch couldn't decipher, like the sign left by someone gone before?

As Dutch came more from the dream, he saw his father differently: Berrigan looked human and nothing else, as if his soul, when Dutch saw him looking down, were perfectly in line with his eyes, and didn't tug heavily against the line of vision. Dutch's own sight, beneath lowered lids, became acquainted with that human image of his father; yet he pretended sleep while Berrigan watched him.

Berrigan looked at his son, intending to bring the young man home, Dutch he'd found alive, emerging from a grove. Berrigan looked sane, and hoped to converse soon, audibly with his son, unwhispering. Berrigan looked, without wavering, more confident in his family now; he nodded toward Dutch, to affirm them all.

A question came, to Dutch: who was his father, who was Berrigan? Now, almost dreaming again, he considered his father's hair might answer.

Berrigan thought that if Dutch would awake he might ask, "Did you know I'd come?" He might joke, "Did the mountains warn you, like preachers?"

Now, for the moment, Dutch, who had pretended sleep, did sleep again and dream: he saw bird wings and fish fins fluttering up like flames of the fire before his closed eyes; behind them, Dutchess bent to someone he couldn't see; her mouth sank down. Then he woke with a start, and quickly rose from the ground.

Berrigan said, "Good morning."

In the firelight, in his father's eyes, as the dawn came dimly, Dutch felt peculiarly visible to himself, as if he saw himself whole for once, and he felt, at that moment, his self was decided on now, though he couldn't recall any decision he'd made, felt some direction, in his life, was affirmed; he was surprised it needed affirmation. He felt precarious, perched, as if he juggled his own life high in a pine top, tossing the pointed brown cones with such skill and confidence, as if all his life were risen into agile fingertips. He was sure his father felt the same about him, recognized his son for what he was.

With interior eyes, Berrigan felt his way into his son's future; yet he could see nothing but a darkness like unknowing, where something could sprout in the life of his son and grow clearer and clearer the more Dutch entered the future; his son seemed, standing up before him out of sleep, like white dough rising out of the now green darkness of dawn.

All this time, before the present light, Berrigan was

vaguely troubled by a dream he couldn't remember until now, a dream of the sun which was like a man floating belly up in the river, as if it had risen gradually from the water, a long red obscurity, the sun's veil. The sun was like a floating man the fish knew intimately; they nibbled with bites like kisses at fingers and toes, sun's cock and nose, at all the bright extremities. From the riverbank, animals looked upon the sun, on someone once familiar who'd become a stranger, one who was no longer theirs, escaping them through the river. The floating sun peered back at the watchers on shore and at Berrigan, stared, as though unseeing, into his ancient animal or human death, floated, distant mote in the ribbon of the world's eye, unwinding, moving on the river like the fabric of his own broadening beam of light.

Berrigan stood in a blindness of the dream, which joined and confirmed the darkness of his knowledge of Dutch: Dutch was like the pupil of his eye. Berrigan imagined him as angel or starlike bird, imagined gills changing to wings to arms probing air or water, and the sky at dawn seemed made of flesh, when Berrigan felt like a tongue exploring the lover's mouth, through his presence in the scene; until he felt his own body probed, urged from within, as if he were a woman elbowed by an interior child.

He thought of trout leaping from the stream, reentering that place they came from, the water where their shadows fell before them; the fish were changed in his eyes, become something else, strangers like the sun he'd dreamed of. Berrigan sucked on his teeth, pulled them long and hard, lingered on their flavor, sealing himself like a secret, sealing the creatures who'd watched the sun in his dream, and the leaping fish, securely, within his interior vision, like parts of the darkness Dutch had appeared in, as life and wake-fulness became full in him. Dutch hadn't spoken yet. They pretended they weren't watching each other, covered their too frequent yawns, and stretched their bodies toward the fire emphatically. Before the dawn, Berrigan had been able to see nothing but the firelight and the prone form of his son; for there'd been no stars, only the blackness of their loss and the loss of the moon behind high clouds. The light came as though to break the clouds.

After a time, Dutch sat back down to warm himself at the fire; his eyes closed again. The new day's light was such that Berrigan remembered how Sawpoot-way's color changed near the birth of their children, like a rose blushes and fades; he remembered her full body, pregnant with the twins, like great fists doubled in her belly; he remembered pain in his head like an old wound, and pain in his upper back, between the blades of his shoulders, as though from head and shoulders something had been removed from him to make him human, to make him less or more than he'd been before; he felt human now. Berrigan remem-bered that pain like a sound he heard this time for the first time, a sound that could only be heard in recall, like someone's voice speaking far from him, familiar and strange. And he felt, in that dawning, that he'd al-most known for sure what he needed to know of his son before the end of their return, that he'd almost known, in something like the way his body felt the morning.

Dutch felt depressed as he sat at the fire; for the re-turn, the journey with his father, had been so une-ventful, too easy, despite the difficulties of ascent; and there wasn't much time left to them, for something important to happen, and nothing was being prepared, no great event he'd been released from Legget for. The certainty in himself, that he'd felt only moments before, had, like the clouds, dissolved with the completion of the dawn; he was disillusioned. No figures swarmed in his mind or in the bright light of day; when he opened his eyes, he would see only the common objects of the scene: the straggling trees and shrubs, the snowline beyond his father's face, the fire between them. When his father spoke, he looked up, eagerly, as if Berrigan's voice in that morning had some answer for him, as if he thought his father knew his future.

His father said, "It's not far now. Shall we go on?"

ALL THAT DAY THE NEARNESS OF THE valley grew upon them; the next day they'd arrive; they approached with anxiety, an unreasoning fear of what they'd find. Berrigan couldn't put any names to his fear; but Dutch moved higher and higher and knew he'd find the valley changed from what it had been to him. It wouldn't be a place he quite belonged, the valley no longer so familiar, his family too distant from him, as if they became strangers. He knew it from the way he felt about his father, and knowledge saddened him. There wasn't anything he intended to do; he entered futility.

Berrigan felt something decisive should have happened in their return, in the journey he now looked back on. Their recent days seemed connected only by the continuous steps they took, each day higher into the range of mountains; the knowledge he'd wished for had never quite come, or if it had, it was knowledge he couldn't appreciate or understand. There'd been his memories, his dreams, things he'd imagined, even thoughts of the future he wasn't used to thinking about, all to show that on the long, physical journey, though nothing of great importance occurred, the mind must be occupied with its own matter, making its own importance out of the trivial items. He wondered if that was what the journey amounted to, just the mind's activity and the arrival home. Now, arriving seemed an anticlimax, as if something important had after all occurred these last few days. What had he expected: Legget to overtake them, a late blizzard? There was nothing to do but walk, and let the mind do what it would, since it would always be doing something, just as his mother had refused to rest about the house of his childhood; she'd found continuous occupation even if his father rested from his heavier labor on the farm. Let it be, without undue worry.

Berrigan didn't know for certain how many days he'd traveled with Dutch, but that day, the next to last, ended, as the others had, and in that night, he dreamed a dream influenced by his nearness to Sawpootway and by the thoughts, dreams, memories, imaginings of recent days; he dreamed while his body, used to its daily exercise, the repetitious steps, seemed to the dreamer to speed homeward in that effortless state, and hope had become as much a part of that body as his lungs, with just that airy pulse of capture and release.

But his dream was different too, from sleep's light and hopeful progress of his body. He dreamed he met me, under a pine tree in those mountains. I wasn't a large man, but slender, wiry, and red-haired. My age, in the dream, was sometimes that of the young man Berrigan knew two decades before; at other times I seemed any age between thirty and fifty; occasionally Berrigan glimpsed a face beyond age, as if I'd entered the apparent permanence of a man well over a hundred. Later my features were more like those of his son than the young man he remembered, but Berrigan always thought of the man in the dream as the first Dutch, Gerhard Blau, and he was glad he could name me. Once he called his friend Fish-out-of-water, as the Indians had.

I said I would enter Berrigan's dreams, and show him what was in his heart, through small, square and flat images Berrigan would recognize as his own dream images. From the mud, I created first a kind of statue, an industrious angel, as busy as Berrigan's mind, whose wings flailed the air like bellows. Sawpootway appeared, out of a cloud bank, and Berrigan, startled and suddenly jealous, stepped back. We behaved as if Berrigan were no longer present, as if he'd retreated into the frame of his dream. Small images in my hands, which Berrigan hadn't seen yet, seemed to urge Sawpootway on; she moved toward them compelled. Berrigan saw that the image maker had made the pictures of her husband, daughter and son; I said they were now immortal. Those images turned before her, as though they were alive within their frames; the images of her family both woke and slept. Sawpootway kissed them with her lips, so eagerly it seemed to Berrigan that she'd consume them. Then she said I was like someone she'd forgotten, and she asked me my name; I wouldn't say any names. She said she thought she recognized me, if she could just place the time. She could call my names. I said not to mind who I was, but to tell me what had become of her, since I'd been gone. So she told her most recent story, of her loss; the tale fell from her mouth, like crumbs from her lips, between the occasional kisses she still gave the images she held, those images of family given. Berrigan never said a word to interrupt; he felt too removed from the scene.

When she'd done with the telling, we agreed to go together for a time; somewhere, I said, as we once might have gone. I pointed to the images of father and son. I said her daughter wasn't there any more. Sawpootway didn't seem to notice it before. Berrigan hadn't. She said Dutchess was free of all this. I asked if I could help her find Dutchess. Sawpootway said she almost remembered what everything was like; yet she had no name for me any more. I said it didn't matter so much that she name me. I said I had a notion where to look for Dutchess. Sawpootway said she'd be grateful.

Eventually, Berrigan woke, shrugged off the dream, incomprehensible and foolish; another day began, the last of that journey and he and Dutch didn't have much to say to each other when they walked. Slowly, through the day, he recalled, as if against his will, more of that night's dream, recalled it as he might a moment of shame.

I'd spoken to Sawpootway of places we might look for the missing child, Dutchess or Dutch; but Berrigan couldn't hear the lowered voice say where those hiding places were. Suddenly, Berrigan, unseen even by himself, though he looked on the scene, through his jealousy, felt excluded even from his own loss, as though the dream allowed him no interest in his missing child, whichever child that was.

I leaned and whispered; held my hands clasped behind my back, my head down, and my shoulder blades stuck out like wings of the angel I'd made and displaced, that angel, masculine, severe, busy angel,

who'd disappeared from the dream, his departure un-
noticed as if he'd never been there, as if the dreamer
had undreamed him, forgotten his existence.

Sawpootway kissed the images of her husband and
son or daughter, their figures reduced to flat forma-
tions of their faces alone: her body swelled out as she
kissed them, and sank as her lips withdrew. I circled
her, to stand out of her sight, hands thrust deep into
my coat pockets as though I held something. I said I
knew many things had fallen in her life, as natural
things fall, like snowflakes, green needles, the fur of
animals, bird feathers, fins, as all fall to earth, down to
the grass blades, as if the world was stirred down by a
god who hid above men like an animal that only
wished to escape them. I said perhaps everything
could be gathered again, as the preachers said.

I said it as though I could fold the world into one
of my pockets, like an injured bird. She turned when I
spoke to her, and my voice, it seemed to Berrigan, had
a new urgency, as it did when I asked her if we should
go now. I spoke, then, almost as though I had to
plead with her, as if she knew and controlled what
we'd do. Behind us, the mountain groaned like a giant
about to move, to walk forth like a man, obliterating
the lesser sound of our human voices, as she answered
me; and I said something else.

Berrigan wondered if we could even hear each
other, beneath the mountain's sound. He wondered if
an avalanche was coming down upon us. The sound
of the mountain was almost visible to Berrigan, as if
he could see his own bones moving against each other
without their flesh cushioning. When no avalanche
came, when there was silence that seemed absolute, he
heard Sawpootway say she was grateful, or I may have
said it. Berrigan watched us descend the slope of a val-

ley; it became like his own, when we sought Berrigan's son, Dutch, or his daughter, Dutchess. In patches of snow we left the unstaggering signature of our descending search, straight and precisely drawn, as if we designed our steps from a previous and fine conception.

Then we were gone and Berrigan appeared again to himself in the dream, so still within the frame, as if he became to himself one of the images I held forth in my hand, an image Sawpootway kissed repeatedly. He saw himself move from stillness and put on an old hat; he'd almost forgotten it, the furry hat with two horns, the buffalo hat. It felt peculiar after so long, out of place on his head after an absence. So he removed it; he breathed more easily. Above a bough of dripping snow, he saw the sun rise like a pool of yellow water. He saw fish in that sun, hovering in place, somehow feminine, trout impatient and afraid like brides waiting in bedrooms for new husbands. The buffalo hat disappeared, forgotten like the angel; Berrigan spread his shoulders wide, as the process of the dream released him to his life again.

Berrigan moved homeward beside his son, and the shame he'd felt that morning when waking had gone, and the fears that had grown during that journey no longer worried him; he only looked forward to seeing Sawpootway and Dutchess, pleased to bring Dutch home to them, when they'd thought him lost.

BERRIGAN AND DUTCH WENT DOWN into the valley, glad to come home. They looked for signs of life; they saw the rooster's movement, the bird pouring up, in feathers, to the cabin roof, like an avalanche in reverse. They came by the creek and passed the cottonwood tree; the hounds appeared around the house, rushing them. Sawpootway stepped from the cabin, a broom in her hand; she swept the bare earth at the edge of the porch. The two men were tired and felt it, wandering long those few un-measured days, as though they'd lived outside of time, confined by mountains, homeless. They saw Sawpoot-way, who hadn't noticed them yet, reverse her broom and lean, as if she'd poke holes for planting in the door's swept earth, or as though the broom, like a crutch, was now meant to support her. When she saw them, she stood straighter than the men who approached. She stared, as if she tried to recognize her men returning.

The day had grown the hottest of the season, and Berrigan's hands, though exposed to the air, sweated as he walked; his pulse felt large in them, swelling out as if his skin would burst, their limits passed by his pulse on each alternate beat, as if everything in him would run out like the hounds to greet someone else, everything in him extended toward the figure staring from the house. Even Dutch, moving ahead, stretched his body toward her, and all Berrigan's life moved through his child. He expected Dutchess to come, as she often had, from cabin or hen house, from the goat ravine with pails, to embrace him; then his blood might return to his body, now almost too harshly poured out. But only the hounds came and reared to place and pound their paws against his chest. He saw, beyond the cabin, that the garden he'd plowed had been worked in his absence; he was grate-ful to Sawpootway and proud. He was moved that work had gone on in his absence. He was released, like Dutch, from capture; and time, so frozen, thawed in his homecoming. He saw someone had written a word he couldn't understand, in French, on the cottonwood bark, large letters hastily cut as if for a sign to someone who followed a trail. He intended to ask Sawpootway what the word meant. Berrigan who, the previous night, had appeared to himself human in dream, let Dutch precede him, the forerunner of his return; for he was patient in his flow, calming the hounds to his heels, speaking their names, "Cinco, Spook, Hasty, Pride." He spoke the animals.

Sawpootway didn't run to them like the hounds. He'd thought, that for this occasion, so singular in their lives, she might move toward them, if slowly, hesitating, like someone who's curious how this strange return comes about. He'd expected she'd put her arms around her son. But she stood, as if Dutch had only been briefly gone, to hunt or fish with his father as usual, as if Legget had never reappeared that spring nor done what he did. When they reached her, she did let the broom fall to the ground, she reached out her hands. She always did that when they came home from a journey of no consequence but food. Dutch took her hands in his, then released them and stepped on the narrow porch. He passed through the doorway. Berrigan kissed her lips swiftly, wondering at the calmness of her smile. He said hello in her language, just as he always did; her reply was usual. He passed her, following Dutch in.

Thurlow lay on his bed, asleep, fully dressed, the black hat beside him, near his hand. His boots and stockings were upon the floor; his coat rested on the back of Berrigan's chair. He expected Sawpootway, who'd entered the room, to tell him who the man was. Instead, as he and Dutch stared at the sleeper, he felt her hand on his arm; he turned toward her. She held out the piece of bark, those signs of animals in wood he'd sent her, marks Dutchess had received instead. He said, "So Adams did come. Good."

She said, "Thank you," in English, and she smiled at him.

Dutch stared at Thurlow, who wasn't wakened by the return of father and son. Berrigan couldn't think how to ask who the stranger was. Sawpootway removed Thurlow's coat and Berrigan sat in his chair. She knelt to remove his boots.

Dutch asked, "Who *is* that?"

"He helped me come home safe." They'd arrived two days before, and Thurlow'd just returned from the river, where he'd been both days, where he'd looked for signs of Dutchess; but she didn't tell them any of that, nor about the note she'd found attached to the bed, fastened with a bone needle. She didn't tell Berrigan yet.

"What are you talking about?" Berrigan asked. "Where did you go, to come back from?"

She told her own story of search and homecoming; but she didn't mention Dutchess. She told the story to her husband, who sat before her unrelaxed, whose feet, horny and large, she brought water to bathe, and told it to her son who stood above them, told it quietly, so not to wake Thurlow.

Thurlow woke anyway, when she was filling in details of their return, woke and nodded to the other men, who nodded in return.

Berrigan asked his name, as politely as he could; it was embarrassing for both the older men.

Thurlow, reddened, leaned forward, and told his name and old preacher's calling, how he'd come far from the East, after wandering the new states and territories; then he listened, intently, while Sawpootway talked, as if he hadn't been with her any of the time she told about, as if he only heard of that time now.

Sawpootway told some things over again. She claimed she knew when Dutch was found, that she'd found him in her own heart, knew he and Berrigan came together. No one argued with her. While she talked, Dutch picked up the piece of bark and he studied its signs, without understanding: the scars around the naked man; the tailed child distorted in form; the rabbit-horse like a strange mule the naked man seemed about to mount; the eagle; the buffalo; the bear; deer-goat; and again the scars, snakelike shapes, those wavy streaks around the man.

Then Sawpootway stopped her talk of her journey, and said, abruptly, "You're hungry."

Berrigan, anxious to ask just one question, dared not ask it yet, but said, "We are." The hounds sat in the shade at the door. He saw them and he saw the last part of the rooster's flight down from the roof, the combed head extended from stiff wings, his brief flurry of landing. Berrigan worked his feet in the basin, his toes kneading the water. Sawpootway rose and embraced her son; his body gave in to hers.

She went to get food for them; but Berrigan couldn't wait any more. He stood up in the water, as Dutch turned with him; he asked, "Where's Dutchess? Where's she gone?"

Dutch looked at his mother, and repeated his father's question, naming Berrigan's fear and his own, "What's happened to her?"

Sawpootway, stopped in the door to the porch, turned toward Thurlow, as if to appeal to him, as if she wanted him to answer and tell them where Dutchess was, but Thurlow, seeing all eyes on him, reddened again; he shrugged and shook his head sadly, as though he felt responsible for their loss. Sawpootway reached into the cotton dress she wore, and the letter Dutchess had written fell before any of the others saw it. Thurlow stood up and looked about for his boots and socks.

Berrigan pointed to the piece of bark in Dutch's hand. He asked, "Didn't Adams give you . . . ?"

Sawpootway stared at the paper on the floor. She said, "It's all I found, except the animals. The word on the tree. It's not a proper word; she didn't write it."

Berrigan almost said Adams hadn't either; Adams didn't know French. "Let me see it," he said.

Thurlow, putting his socks on, said, "I must be going. I just needed that little rest. So I've got to go." No one paid attention to him; they didn't watch as he slipped by Berrigan and Sawpootway, by Dutch who'd come to look over his father's shoulder, and he passed through the door, boots and hat in hand. But Thurlow, having entered this valley, couldn't think of anywhere in the world to go, and soon the three within the house, no longer so absorbed in Dutchess's careful script, heard him outside, chopping the wood.

IT WAS MORNING IN THEIR CAMP, NOW far from the valley, when Dutchess asked Adams, "Are you sure? We could still go back. Tell them so they could see us tell them."

He shook his head. The sorrel snorted, out of sight around some rocks. For three days they'd remained in the same place, preparing to enter the badlands of the Arkansas. The first day out, they'd re-encountered the hunters; the three men apparently waiting for them, that meeting on the river planned; and Dutchess and

Adams had traveled the rest of that day, and camped through the night, with them.

The men, especially the big one named Marais, seemed eager to talk, in their broken English. Dutchess had asked, after hearing how they'd met her mother, what Legget was like. Marais said Legget was a *determined* fellow, and he repeated the big word; the other two repeated it to each other, laughing together. But the hunters were uneasy with Dutchess; she intruded upon stories they'd already made, ruined their jests. Adams felt their presence as a threat, stood prepared to defend her. He took Dutchess away the next morning, soon as he felt he could. He led the sorrel stallion Dutchess rode. The large hunter, Marais, who was even bigger than Adams, had asked, once as they went, if she really was Marie's daughter, and Berrigan's.

Adams had answered for her. "Yes," he said.

Silently, as they rode, the two other hunters, whose names no one had caught, who were Cantrieux and Azul, prepared their altered stories of the girl for the campfires, jokes to edge into future ears. Marais was only interested in the mother now. He'd told Dutchess and Adams all the story Marie had told, and he repeated it, as if he hadn't believed what he'd just said. They asked that he repeat certain details, for he filled the tale and his English with French words and phrases they couldn't understand.

Now it was a morning in their own camp, where the river began to spread toward the flatter land. They drank their morning coffee slowly, in silence; they pulled on the dried meat with their teeth. Dutchess jerked her head up to a sound in the brush, and asked who was there. It was only a jack rabbit running away from them, and her voice, which she alone heard, ripped like a fire through the sleep she'd had. She knew she woke them.

When the sun was a little higher, while they still lingered, as if they'd remain in that place another day, Dutchess said, "So this is what it's like."

"What?"

"Eloping." When Adams looked, she continued, "I don't even know what's become of my brother, whether he's alive or dead, or anything, and I never dreamed I'd do anything like this to him, not to him, never, and I've gone from my father, and my mother's off going around crazy somewhere, and the place that's always been home." By then she was giggling; her voice had risen. Adams didn't understand that change. She said, "There was that tree . . . Dutch and I used to climb in, and the treehouse." Adams just nodded. He'd heard it or something like it, without her new giddiness, every day. "Once I hid above him, and I was quiet, a little animal. I shook the needles down around him. No, they were leaves, not needles. Where did the needles come from? He didn't know I was there, not yet, and I laughed when he found out."

Adams said, as he hadn't said before, "That's all behind you now. You'll see, it will be better."

And Dutchess believed him; but she laughed at him, full-voiced, no giggling now but still from the same mood. "Yes, my husband has come. You came and got me; someone did come. What do you suppose she'd say?" Adams knew she meant her mother, who'd spoken so much to her daughter about an old time of loneliness and fear.

Before they'd left the hunters, those three men had organized a kind of wedding banquet, with deer meat, wild berries, fish, coffee, a little chokecherry wine. The hunters had all been jealous, even Marais, who was reminded of Marie by Dutchess. They'd invented someone to love; but the loved one had come before them with another; all their parables of hens and cock, candles and hounds, were struck down by Adams, by his presence; the old jokes couldn't mean the same thing any more; the girl who'd been hidden from them, even from Adams, had come with this man. Dutchess and Adams had touched tin cups of wine together, solemnly, before they drank. The three hunters slapped their own thighs and each other's shoulders; they shook hands with Adams and kissed Dutchess roughly as if they were afraid of her.

Many days had passed since that night, and now Dutchess, under the rising sun, said, "They won't find the letter." She'd said that before too.

Adams, this time, only said, "Sure they will."

She said, "When they get into bed. They won't bother much about us now, I guess."

Adams said, again, "They know where we'll settle. They'll find the letter, and they'll find us if they want. You told them what they need to know; you wrote it down."

"Yes, I wrote it down for them."

"He can read it, your father can, even if she can't. And your brother can read it too. He'll come home, and he can read it too."

"He'll come home."

"Sure," Adams said. He had his own feelings of guilt, about their departure, and didn't like it when she talked about her brother, especially about her brother.

Those three hunters had worried her so; she didn't like how they looked at her. Especially the two whose names she hadn't understood, who'd laughed so much together as though they alone shared a dirty secret;

they'd seemed to come into her life, surreptitiously, like worms called up by the spring thaw. They weren't men to her, not even Marais, but alien forces of nature. There was something underground, something she couldn't quite stand, even about Marais, as if he were just, as she made him now, filling her metaphor, a larger worm than the others, and the worms had become hunters on horseback, with long blue guns dug out of the earth; and when those men spoke among themselves they talked wildly into the dark face of dreams she didn't have or know.

They were absolute strangers; their dreams rose over their heads, dark clouds, and they spoke as though they thought their own voices, in that foreign tongue, could decipher the message of features they saw on those dream-dark puffs. The clouds of their dreams were made by their voices, and their voices could never hear what their own voices said to make dreams, those large puffs of cumulus, dark with white tails stuck in three mouths.

She remembered how Marais sneezed at the banquet they'd arranged, and it seemed her own dreams must dissipate; they mistook her for someone else, that's what it was. They would dissipate her dream of a life for her herself; they would, in this wedding party she hadn't chosen, and she would never fully return to herself. Their huge, cloudy dreams might destroy her.

She knew they didn't like Adams, though he'd been a companion of theirs, and had for two years traveled the long way to the mountains with them. As they'd talked, it seemed to her it would have made more sense if they'd spoken to their horses and mules. She was arriving at some new conception of herself, in her life with Adams. She didn't know what life would be yet.

Once Marais had looked at her, over the fire, and he'd moved his hand, like an awkward paw, over his eyes, as if he meant to clear a cobweb, or wipe off a vision he couldn't endure. Then he spoke something about her mother; she thought he was crying, as if the smoke troubled his eyes. She pitied him that one time and that was why, sometimes in her thoughts, she looked upon him differently from the others.

"Who were those men to me?" she wondered, aloud to Adams. She meant, who were they to worry her memory? "As if they were a family I lost."

Adams knew she meant the hunters, though she hadn't mentioned them for days. They no longer had any description in his mind. They'd become vaporous, those old companions who spoke a language he poorly understood. They affected him disagreeably now, as if, through his love for Dutchess, his friends had become his enemies. But he and Dutchess were far from them; they were only the smoke from the fire, rising to disappear, as he threw on dust and the remains of their coffee, the hunters' gift.

Dutchess watched what he did. It didn't mean they wouldn't stay; for he'd done the same each of three days. But this time, when the flames were out, thin smoke no longer visible, he stood above her, and she knew he'd remain until she answered. So she rose to say, "Yes, I'm ready enough now." And she was that ready this time, ready enough to think she'd have her own life with him, whatever it might be, good and evil, and she believed she'd thoroughly fallen out with that valley of her family.

She began to prepare the pack he would carry on

his shoulders, the one he'd borne when she saw him that first time, coming to the garden where she planted the beans. She began to feel glad of that quarrel with an old life; now she felt physically incapable of returning. She felt glad of some new, more complicated person she couldn't describe, that she knew she was already becoming. Adams wiped the dust from his hands. She took his fingers, and pressed them hard into her lips. She thought she might say he was her husband, and say it seriously, without mocking her mother's talk about husbands coming or not coming for their potential wives. Instead she asked him, "Can we go now?"

Adams laughed happily, certain only now that she wanted to go on. "Sure," he said.

She thought they'd be another family, not some old one that couldn't ever be what she wanted; but Adams wouldn't have understood that. She couldn't think why she thought he wouldn't understand.

He said, "There's where we go." He pointed toward the east, and they went that way, in the direction her parents had turned from years before; he pointed from the mountains, dwindling toward badlands, then plains, then prairie, toward the trader's city at the meeting of two rivers, Mississippi and Missouri.

SAWPOOTWAY ENTERED THE CHICKEN house at dusk; the cock and hounds followed at her heels, as if she were Dutchess. She moved from nest to nest, taking eggs by the light of her lantern. It was dark under the long shadow of western mountains, already night in the hen house. She didn't hurry, for there wasn't any reason to hurry; she could still find her goats in the dim light, and milk them in the total darkness. Slow and preoccupied in all recent days, she lingered at her gathering, probing the darkness, with her light and her fingers, for the whiteness of eggs.

She came from the hen house at last, as from some half sleep like the dusk, in which she'd long revolved, came out as though from water where dark bodies gradually turned. She returned toward the house, where she'd seen Dutch earlier, in the fading light, watching her enter the hen house door. He'd gone. The rooster advanced beside her; the hounds remained patient at her heels, long slinking bodies like part of the darkness.

Berrigan looked up from oiling his gun. He sat in his chair under two candles, while Thurlow, moving quickly out of her chair, watched her face. Berrigan smiled and went on with his work; his big hands, in the candlelight, gentle on the wood and metal parts, as if they were part of his body.

Thurlow said, "The fire needs building." The fire didn't need any help, but he went there and knelt. All day he'd been cutting trees, to build himself his own shelter in the western end of the valley, beyond the horses and mule. Dutch and Berrigan had helped him, over his protests.

She went out again, with the pails for milking, though the goats this time of year wouldn't have, in their condition, two full pails to give; it was her habit to take two pails. She walked toward the western rise of ground, and found Dutch had gathered the two goats for milking, hobbled them near the water, anticipating his mother's need. He stood near as she knelt; he held the lantern for her. The four hounds lay down like shadows and the rooster scratched grass out of the dirt, sending blades and dust up in a cloud. Sawpootway pulled the teats long to squirt milk, and relaxed them, again squeezed her fingers like hard rings to pulse them, and she had the rhythm of the milking. She said, "You want to talk?" She didn't look up, the side of her face pressed against the distended side of the pregnant goat as if she listened to the kid within.

"Yes," he said. Dutch wasn't surprised that she asked, nor that she spoke in his father's language; she'd spoken so for days now, ever since his return. He watched her fingers relax and squeeze, now more untender on the teats, watched the pregnant nannies standing calm, as if they were indifferent both to their loss and to the release of their too great fullness. He said, "She left us that letter, saying what she did." He knelt down beside her, held the light nearer. He didn't have to speak as loud as he did when they'd been separated by his standing height. "I'd like to find her."

"She went on her own. You cannot care about her going any more."

"Well, I'd like to see her. I'd like to go."

Sawpootway stopped her milking and looked up at him. "It's not you want to see her." He didn't contradict her. Behind him, in the west, she saw a series of peaks that looked like an angular woman's body lying down; a star stood over one breast, as if to mark it for future reference. The mountain woman's arms, below the jutting shoulders, were invisible like her features, the countenance in darkness. Her body was described only by the dim aureole of a sun that had set. It was nearly dark now, and Sawpootway peered toward the human obscurity of Dutch's face outside the circle of the light. She asked, "*Why* go?" She thought she knew why.

"To go," he said. He wanted to add something, but couldn't think of the words. He looked away from her and studied the red cock and the blue and white hounds; he moved the light; animals and their colors were swallowed up by the darkness beyond its ring of light. He watched her work again, saw the milk spurt, and he remembered fruit seen that morning, fallen from a tree that grew in the wide end of that valley; and he remembered, from a former time, when he was very young, that fruit fallen like the goat milk, pears he and Dutchess found on the earth. His mother took the last of that goat's milk. Dutchess, with her long mouth curved, smiling, had come up to him, and picked the wild pear from the ground; joking, she'd bitten into the side it rotted on, the side that lay against the earth.

Dutch frowned at his memory. His mother rose toward the other goat, bearing her pails; the pail she'd used had so little milk in it that her body wasn't pulled down to that side. She looked again at that, now darker, figure in the west and what had seemed to her a woman's body now seemed a sleeping man. Cock and hounds, goat, seemed indifferent to her action. She felt she might take on the indifference of animals, and she laughed, shortly, a laugh like a rasping cough. When she looked at Dutch again, her hands working the teats, she said, from that new mood, "You would just go."

Dutch hesitated, then nodded reluctantly. When he'd come home and found Dutchess gone, her absence became the thing he was expecting, and he knew his own course was decided.

Sawpootway took the lantern; Dutch didn't go with her. In the east, the stars struck down in long streaks of light, hard from the sky, bright, material bodies intruding upon soft darkness, inhuman streaks to pierce their valley lives, to descend like white needles into her heart; those stars seemed so close, as if she could reach out and pluck them, like fruit, from the stem-like beams. The stars would be alive in her hands like small birds, their tiny hearts pulsing in her palm; she felt she could make their death, and might make death now, in near indifference, after the talk with her son.

Then the valley broke darkness over her extended fingers, over her eyes; the sun had gone; she'd set the buckets and the lantern down for a moment, still far from the house. She saw the house, the dim light of the candles through the window. Thurlow, always so tired after their journey, probably slept, where he bedded near Dutch, in Dutchess's absence. The moon would rise soon, dimming the influence of stars.

The rooster left her when she continued; he went toward the hen yard. She let the hounds, who seemed to know her desire, follow her into the cabin; they crawled, beseechingly, upon their bellies, through the doorway. When she sat down in her chair, the pails beside her, two dogs huddled down at her feet.

Sawpootway picked her sewing up. Berrigan brought her two candles. She looked at the sewing in her lap, patterns become almost meaningless in the leather, like a message she couldn't decipher any more, as if they'd been designed by someone else and never known her stitching hands; she saw her own lap and her knees, and the two hounds, Cinco and Spook, sleeping with muzzles near her feet.

Berrigan lit three more candles near her, since she did nothing yet; so five lights flared in the cabin, like wings flung up from branchless trunks, from the candle stems. Carefully, her fingers felt out the threaded designs of animals, as if she still couldn't see them. She wondered why the designs were there, patterns that only made her think of her father: once he'd moved like a young god of the plains; now he burned up in her mind, his body that she'd tried to restore after death, his flesh consumed in the sky like a shooting star; fire wreathed his stitched and darkening body; a mule flew before him, and a bear followed with snakes in its mouth, animal backs and his own back hulking in departure, into the darkness she'd seen that night.

Sawpootway laid her sewing down and accidentally

dropped the needles of bone; they rattled and danced on the wooden floor. She stared into the fire across the room. She was alone with Berrigan: Thurlow slept and Dutch hadn't yet come in from the night.

Her husband stood above her, the middle of his body among the candles, his face in darkness. He saw her wince repeatedly, blinking as if the five lights of candles hurt her eyes. He asked her, "Did he tell you?" But Sawpootway slept, or pretended. Berrigan, bending into the light, couldn't be sure. He spread fur upon her, tucked it around her. Above the dark animal hair, her face seemed too white for any human face. Then he knew she slept. For, in her sleep, she did a familiar thing, muttered that old language of hers, he'd learned at her will, that their children had been born to. Sawpootway spoke confused fragments of scenes from their previous life. He knew she spoke, not to him, but to the spirit of her father.

She spoke of their passage to these mountains, of the plains and her father's death, of one she hadn't allowed her love to, of the children she'd conceived, and taken to mountains, to take possession, through a child, of the religion of her tribe. She told of that elopement with Berrigan to the mountains the tribe once lived in and had still returned to sometimes in her childhood, how they came in the wagon leaving stolen gold behind.

While she defended her life to her father, Berrigan watched her face: she descended far into her own past, lay in her childhood, after her speech in defense of elopement, lay among bushes, very small and speechless, while her parents searched for her, while they pretended she was lost or hadn't yet been given, been born, to them, when her cries were for a husband who never seemed to come.

She seemed more haunted than ever by past life. Berrigan thought it was from that he'd saved her; and he wondered if he'd been wrong to take her, after the death of her husband and father. He looked down at the hounds, long heads across her feet as though they'd comfort her in those dreams.

SAWPOOTWAY SAID SHE WAS; SHE WAS hungry, her breath audible in release as she came from the creek. Dutch had gone, but only for the day's hunting, and she and Berrigan had bathed in the chilly water. He squatted under the tree preparing the little fire, and she squatted down too, her hands smoothing water from her belly, stuck forward against the warmth. The two trout he'd caught by hand, to her pleasure and girlish shrieks, lay between them on a clean cloth once part of a dress.

Though it was the hottest day yet, she shivered and hugged herself, as though her body would escape control. She reached for Berrigan's shirt and slipped it on; it was far too large and fell, as she knelt, over her thighs and knees, only her toes showing beneath the hem. She put on his hat, and pulled its brimless fur edge down over her eyes. "Look at me," she said. She spread her arms and smiled. "Look, I'm like a man." She pushed the headpiece back with her thumb, to see what he was doing.

Berrigan saw her mouth slack, wide with desire, but he turned to the fish. One fish lay opened, its interior on view, and he slit the other one's belly. He saw she peered, as if in approval of her food, and she fixed the first fish on the prepared stick. They both held sticks of fish to the fire, and were careless, looking at each other long, so the meat was scorched.

It was noon when they ate, and there were no shadows; then small thin shadows grew slenderly, darkness edging from light, as the moon grows from nothing but previous darkness. There were two mountain jays in the small green leaves of the cottonwood; the birds plucked among the boughs for nesting matter. They seemed very familiar to Berrigan, as everything in the scene did, within their intimacy; especially the birds conveyed a good past life, or were harbingers of a good future. He watched, and didn't fear, their pecking, sharp beaks.

And he watched Sawpootway; sometimes the hat fell again, over her eyes like a veil. The rooster flew up into the cottonwood and the jays scattered, as Sawpootway and Berrigan laughed to see that flutter of bird arrival and escape. The rooster recalled Dutch and Dutchess. Berrigan said, "I think he'll go soon, now." The sun was out, no longer obscure, and he shaded his eyes to look up at the rooster. He said, "I'm afraid so."

Sawpootway laughed, surprising Berrigan, and she said, "They're hiding. They flew off. Like the jays to hide and look at us." Her smile was wide and teasing under the edge of his hat brim.

The shade edged out from beneath the bodies of the hounds, dark liquid leaking after noon. Berrigan turned to the east, and saw the sentinel peaks, the snowline climbing higher each day.

Sawpootway indicated his hat, and his shirt; she asked, "You know me?" She pulled the shirt of animal patterns closer about her.

"Yes," he said. "Well. I know you well enough." He loved her, whatever they or their children came to, whoever might, like birds, hide and watch them naked or nearly so, eating their fish.

Sawpootway, deepening her voice, said, "I'm Dutch now. Look." She laughed at her pretense. When Berrigan didn't seem willing to share the joke, to take part in her mood, her mouth fell under the shade of the hat's brim, and she was afraid she'd harmed him, in some way she couldn't quite identify, except by a previously unacknowledged injury, self-inflicted, of her own, the wound that had moved her to this disguise.

But Berrigan's fingers, as if aware of her distress, caressed the place where her lips met over her teeth. And he slid back the hat, to reveal her forehead; her hair fell out as dark as the shadows creeping from under the bodies of hounds. Her tongue turned against the tips of his fingers, slippery, like a fish.

She asked again, in a small voice, unconfident, "Do you know me?"

He felt her tongue, like the child of her mouth, and she sucked the tips of his fingers, which lay across the hard edge of her teeth. "Yes," Berrigan said. "Well enough." But, with his free hand, he removed the hat entirely, and studied her broad, bony features as if for the first time. The hand that had uncovered her head lay around her neck, and his fingers felt her pulse swell and fall against his own. He felt so near and so far. A few small buds from the tree lay on the ground; perhaps the rooster or the jays had knocked them down, buds with leaf shapes edging out in spring.

Recently, Sawpootway remembered, she had dreamed, repeatedly, of fallen fragments, thin peels of flesh, skin like leaves, as if slender knives had flayed her flesh, like her father's, and that was the harm come into her life. She said to herself that there was only the shower of simple water, refreshing their lives, a waterfall they stood in together. She'd hoped that nothing would ever harm her son, and she'd felt all the world answered her hope, but for the needles of pine trees in dreams, reluctant to agree with her will; she'd dreamed of a prickling in her throat. She felt her neck beat to Berrigan's fingers, knew her pulse, when he felt her.

It was the image of Adams that preoccupied Berrigan for the moment, between their bathing and the next act of their love, of Adams embracing Dutchess, his daughter going soft, as Dutch couldn't be soft to Berrigan. Sawpootway, under his fingers, melted like the winter, like the mountain, while he imagined his daughter with Adams. He laid Sawpootway back on the ground. Berrigan entered the thaw; his eyes felt the sun entering the nearby water, as if it were thirsty like the hounds. Their dogs didn't heed Berrigan and Sawpootway; they licked their paws in the shade, and snapped at flies. Berrigan and Sawpootway moved on Berrigan's shirt.

When he felt his climax approach, Berrigan fought it, even after he passed any chance of control, contended as he might against his death, not because he didn't want that ecstasy, but to increase the moment, to tear out of himself, beyond and against his own will. In the thick pulse, within her body, he didn't know what she looked like any more, as if his eyes had no importance in the world he'd entered.

He knew nothing of her from the act, only the blindness of that moment, as though a dark body overcame his own, some strange flesh like their joined bodies, the instant of his pulse torn from him, and now this relaxation, separation beginning, while he diminished. He didn't want to know her; what more would it mean, to understand the woman? She lay on her back, upon her animal designs, and drew her knees farther up, pulling slightly aside as Berrigan withdrew.

She no longer sewed the designs that lay beneath her; nor did she speak her old tongue; for that language grew too much a part of the childhood days of Dutch and Dutchess; now she would release them to their father's will for them. Berrigan was the one she thought bore them away from their old lives, just as he moved from her after love-making. But for the first time in years, she felt she might have conceived a new child, or eased the way to do it later, and she couldn't decide whether she wanted such a child; she didn't quite believe in the possibility any more.

Berrigan said, "You see. There are some things, after all." He leaned from his elbow to nuzzle her features, again familiar to his eyes. "Some good things about not having the children." And he pointed around them, so she'd be certain to notice their scene: the trees, the dogs, stream, mountains, their own presence, alone. Her lips were dark from their recent act, and Berrigan grazed there, without his former desire; it was that usual familiarity he wished to acknowledge with small kisses, the recognition of her face, renewed through the recent act.

Berrigan lay back, keeping only the touch of his calf on hers or of his thigh on her thigh. He looked through the tree branches, at the sky, clear but for the tree and the rooster and the sun. The bird tucked his head under a wing, then removed it, beat the air with uncropped wings, and flew. Berrigan watched the extended flight over his head, the bird returning toward the hen yard. He said, "It's good here, by ourselves."

Soon they'd dressed and the tree's shadow reached their clothed bodies and fell over them like the sleep they felt so close to. When Sawpootway looked at Berrigan, his eyes were closed, his breathing as slow as a hibernating animal's. She raised herself on an elbow and smiled on the still features. She rose and went to the creek, only to gather water and return. All the water she'd tried to hold leaked through her fingers, but she moved her damp palms over his eyes and his forehead. When Berrigan opened his eyes, from pretended sleep, her smile became a harsh laugh. He held her again, as if he might renew the sexual act, but he remained still, his embrace meant only to confirm, in that sleepy tenderness, the act's significance, the ligaments that bound them. She asked him, "He will go?"

She didn't require his answer, and he didn't feel prepared for any such speech. They lay toward each other as he held her.

She said, "Sometimes, sometimes, I have too much, more than enough." She wasn't weeping yet, and he didn't know how she meant that, till she said, "What child is worth this?" And her tears were visible when she continued; her words came rapidly, as if she hadn't time any more to think of them, English words, easily, as if she'd always known them, "I don't know revenge, what revenge, but it would be sweet. I would be careful and clever; I would be subtle."

She would be, Berrigan thought, as meticulous and subtle as the designs she'd made before; only the material designed would be different. But he didn't believe in her revenge, that it was in her now. Who could she take such revenge on? It was just her talk to him and to her, the talk she needed more than the tears. He rose and took her up by her arms; he raised her as gently as he'd lift an egg in his palm; and, though no terrible burden, her body seemed reluctant to leave that place, that scene of their freedom from children, beneath the cottonwood where the birds had been; and they passed from the creek under the sun, words they'd spoken invisible in the temperate air, and the eaten fish now invisible but for bone remains and the small scraps. The loud jays were only memories in the branches, and the rooster had flown, that recent time now something left in part behind them, like so much else in their lives: Berrigan remembered how she'd knelt, as the fish roasted over the fire, the graceful woman, poignant; how she was veiled under his hat brim; how his fingers lingered in her mouth as she sucked, as if for life, and he'd felt and seen the blue-white edges of her teeth, a few of them missing or broken and sharp to his fingertips.

Guiding her, he entered the door, remembering, and he felt a vague uneasiness in his loins; for the valley seemed to arrive and depart with the mountain: these things, so familiar to him, now both going and coming, as if, as he entered their house, he went out; or, in memory, he'd entered Sawpootway and departed too. So Dutchess might come again to the valley, returning on herself, back into the body she'd known as a child, the future body moving through the past; or, in leaving them as she had, she might bring them to her at some future time, drawing them, as they entered the house, toward the distant place by the two rivers, to the trading place he'd known as Pain Camp more than two decades before. So he felt then that Dutchess drew them toward what he'd come to know as the rind of his own world of the mountains, something shucked off from this valley core. Except for his own few trips to Santa Fe the only word of that world had come to him recently, with the trappers, hunters who'd come upon the valley the summer before: Marais, Cantrieux, Azul, Legget, and Adams, and now the lost preacher who'd come too far for any congregation.

When Sawpootway sat down in her chair to stare at the walls, Berrigan felt so tired and confused he lay down on their bed. He thought again, almost unwillingly, of Dutchess returning, her image rising up so naturally as he lay down. He imagined she held eggs in her palm; her image was still, frozen in that act. Then he saw himself among busy, muddy streets; he heard the noise of other men, traders in the growing town, busy as if they'd trouble and exercise their lives without relaxation, despite drinking and brawling and the few women, those mostly Indian.

He slept and dreamed: Dutch and Dutchess returned together to the valley, and found nothing, after Sawpootway and he, drawn after their children, had disappeared out of the time they'd known twenty years; Dutch and Dutchess found no image of father or mother under renewed noon light, no signs but those of their brief intercourse under the tree, of their hardness and softness in the pressed grass, small signs of the eaten fish, scattered bones, bones Dutch lifted to reveal the marks beneath, signs of parental sex. Dutchess wailed and spread her body on the crushed grass, and she stroked her grief's pattern, the shape of a bird or an angel moving on earth, obliterating the parent signs with her own body's flailing mark. She slept and Dutch watched her through that night.

When it was morning, Berrigan's son looked about him, and the shadow of the mountain, retaining the night, fell from the east onto his sister's body, still spread on the earth like the shadow of a bird, and fell on the invisible signs of parents and fish. There were pools of dew on the ground when Dutch put his fingers on his sister's eyes. He still peered about, intently, as if he hoped to discover the presence of parents after all, or the trail they'd left, afraid he'd missed some additional small mark, beyond the visible sign of his sister's sleep, that would describe the departure of their mother and father.

AT EVENING, SAWPOOTWAY AND BER-rigan went to the creek again, revisiting the scene of a time that now seemed special to Berrigan, a turning point, where they'd been transformed in a way they couldn't quite recognize yet. Dutch and Thurlow hadn't returned, and weren't even expected till the next day or the next. The air had cooled some, but was still temperate and soothing, and there was no breeze in the evening. Berrigan stood with one hand on the tree bark, looking down at the woman huddled to herself by his feet as if she were cold in the gentle weather, her arms wrapped about her knees, her eyes invisible till she bent back her head and spoke to him. She asked, "Is he like Legget?"

It was light enough to see her upturned face. Frowning, he said, "You were wrong about who Legget was."

"But Adams?" She looked over the water.

"I don't know much about him. Only he came this year, like last, and I saw him out on his own while I was looking, and knew nothing bad of him. I wanted to let you know how I was, that I was looking." So Berrigan had trusted the man, Adams, to take his message, had trusted he'd arrive in the valley on his way somewhere else, bearing the word he couldn't read.

"No more?"

"Nothing you don't know. I guess he had a mother and father, like anybody else does." Berrigan laughed, to break the tension in her voice, and she did smile briefly, face upturned, at his small joke. "He's young, younger than the others. He seemed decent enough." He looked toward the mountains. "I guess Dutchess liked him."

Again, Sawpootway lowered her face and looked over the water, toward the southern mountains, then toward the twin-peaked height where Berrigan looked. Once, sitting so, under a different tree, the lodge-pole pine, she'd studied the trapper across the river, and studied the mule that gazed back at her. All eyes, even Berrigan's, had been on her then. She'd thought how Berrigan met Legget while fishing; but when she'd come, there'd been no fish cutting through the air nor the net rising heavy with trout; the pool had swirled and surged on past them; the sun had cut sharply down to heat them in the thaw. From their mouths that chilly morning, their words had seemed heavy, physical bodies. She had made a fool of herself, not of Legget; she should have listened to Berrigan; Berrigan should have stopped it. She had even asked Legget if he'd ever had a woman. She felt foolish now, to have asked such things. What had overcome her? He hadn't even been a Frenchman; she knew that now. And she said it, by accident, aloud, "He wasn't even a Frenchman."

Berrigan knew what she meant. He said, "No, he wasn't." Legget wasn't her old husband, LeGuey; Berrigan had killed that husband, when LeGuey'd come for Berrigan with the knife, along with Smith and

Thomson. Berrigan no longer remembered the killing, not the act, if he'd ever remembered; but he'd
fought, alongside the half-breed, fought three men,
and one had been LeGuey. All three lay dead afterwards, bodies scattered around a little rise of ground.
Legget was not LeGuey: Sawpootway had seen her
husband, and Smith and Thomson, buried by Berrigan
and me. She and the half-breed, Pawkittew, had
watched, with the half-breed's mule.

Now Berrigan bent down, raised her face, and
kissed her on the high cheekbone, gently, as if he
thought she must be consoled for his own memories.
He remembered how he'd loved her when she was
pregnant.

She said, "I asked him if she was an Indian girl."

Berrigan released her face. Clouds gathered above
like words they'd once spoken and must repeat now.

Sawpootway said, "I should have let him. It would
have been as good. Now Dutch will be gone too."

"No." Berrigan hesitated to say more, not really
knowing what his denial meant; and he didn't want to
surprise her too much from her own reasons and or-
dering of the past. He did want to know if she'd ever
really believed Legget to be her old, dead husband.
And if she did believe that, who then, to her, was
Adams? And how could the past have become, in
these mountains, such a nightmare?

She said, "You didn't like it. You didn't like the
trick." She thought, though, that Dutch, disguised,
her foolish deception, could only have fooled a lover's
unseeing eyes; she couldn't be held responsible. She'd
never meant the trick to work, had she? "Something
else moved me to it, something past, like my father's
hand." She stopped to think about that idea, of her
dead father's hand on her life; she hadn't known she

would say anything like it. "Why didn't you stop me, then?" She looked up at Berrigan, curiously, and, when he reddened in the last light, and turned his head away, she rose up to put her hands over his mouth, wanting no answer. "Do you remember how we touched, when we danced, when we met?"

He nodded his head, making no effort to remove her hands; he would let her move them herself. He remembered well, and he touched her, through the cloth she'd put on that afternoon, as he'd touched her then; and she moved her hands from his mouth and touched him as she'd touched him then, as they'd first touched each other intimately in the dance she'd taught him, in the wood outside her husband's cabin.

She felt his cock stir to her touch. She said, "I came to you like a surprise." Even then it had seemed to her that something other than her own will moved her toward him, in her husband's house, when Berrigan had come with Smith and Thomson, and with the younger man, with me; she'd tried me, to check that other will, had lain with me after Berrigan, beside the great river.

Berrigan, after a long silence, said, "Yes, it may have been like that." But he was thinking of Legget again. Legget must have followed their arguing departure with his eyes, as Sawpootway left the river after Berrigan.

Still touching her, beneath the waist, he looked up quickly toward the mountain; for, from the corner of his eye, he thought he'd glimpsed something moving through the peaks. He decided it was only some deformation of the fading light. Yet he retained the figure, disappearing between the white horns, like a mote in his eye, and he sighed, with an irretrievable loss, becoming reconciled to a sense of failure, now one child was gone from the touch of his body and the other was going soon. He'd closed his eyes and Sawpootway, stretching, risen on tiptoe, licked his eyes with her tongue. Berrigan rubbed her through the thin cloth. He remembered she'd worn cloth when they'd met, when they'd danced in the clearing.

He saw the figure of Legget, as he must have been after he and Sawpootway had gone from sight: Legget must have squatted and rubbed his brow, waiting for Dutchess. Did clouds cover the two peaks, blending them to one figure of cloud pierced by peaks and sunlight? A female figure, embodying all the trapper's hope, must have disappeared; and clouds must have left him, clouds like those rising now toward the peaks above Berrigan and Sawpootway, laying down shadows like eagle wings. How would Legget be, after what they'd done to him, after he'd released Dutch?

And the image came to Berrigan, with the question, as if long prepared to appear in that moment: Legget laughed harshly into the palm of his hand, never to be reconciled to his pain; he rubbed his dampened hand on his pants leg. His light hair had grown so long now; he felt it between rubbing fingers. He was caged in the mountains; but now he could remember, without so much hatred, the son approaching to deceive him. He thought he'd almost released himself from the madness that kept him among the images of Berrigan's family. But the images held him as fast to mountains as ever.

And Legget held fast to his memory: a figure *had* appeared, as from his dream of his future life, a figure, though deceiving, in white veil and dress, like a promised bride, ridiculous image detached from his dream, as if the pupil had come loose from his eye; and the figure *had* come to Legget when the man and woman disappeared. Legget knew now that the dress and veil had been brought from Santa Fe, on Sawpootway's insistence, long after the birth of her children; she wanted the wedding garment to confirm their life in the valley. Legget knew because he heard Sawpootway's voice, disembodied, addressing him in dreams, explaining herself, her own obsessions that so troubled him with deceptions; and he suspected the girl had not been his own dream at all, but something forced upon him by some alien god, belonging, perhaps, to the Indians who hung on the canyon walls, or to Sawpootway's ancestors. In dream, Legget heard her voice, guessed at her maternal figure in the white dress, her features behind the veil, and he imagined Sawpootway's desire for Berrigan, that Berrigan himself saw when she interrupted his reverie with speech, desire imprinted on her face with its own pattern, like one of her old designs in leather.

Sawpootway, pulling his hand after her, said, "Come in, before it's dark."

THAT NIGHT THE FIRE BURNED HIGH; Berrigan's bed felt soft and dark, dry and warm, and he rested, as Sawpootway's voice wove through the house. She said, "She might have expected someone to come; I did once."

Berrigan said, "I know, and no one came when they were supposed to. Then LeGuey did."

"He wasn't afraid of you, this Adams wasn't. He wasn't afraid to take her, to touch her here." Adams, she thought, hadn't believed Dutchess poisonous and too foreign for a human touch. LeGuey was taught Sawpootway was poisonous by her own father, the poisoner; but even LeGuey hadn't believed that, and Berrigan never even entertained the thought. Now no woman would need to console Dutchess for the loss of men, as the tribeswomen had consoled Sawpootway when her first bleeding ended and she exited, without a husband, from the hut. This Adams entered when the parents were gone, had come bringing a message from one parent to another, intercepted by Dutchess; and he'd taken her swiftly as if he were certain of his life and love. "He took her with a sureness." Adams hadn't nosed about like a ferret for rabbits, didn't trade with them for her. He left nothing in exchange; Dutchess left the letter. No, he'd brought no bright metallic objects into barter.

Berrigan looked out through the eastern window, the window Adams had recently watched the hunters through; but he could see nothing in the darkness, sensed only the presence of twin peaks before his face. He closed his eyes and felt, in the woman's distant past, receding plainsland, the curve of horizon all around; tiny suns multiplied behind his lids, filling the landscape's sky, suns like coins of gold with images of Sawpootway stamped upon them. He saw her land again.

Sawpootway remembered that Berrigan hadn't drunk with her father as her first husband had: Snakesnorter was dead and rendered when they came. At first she hadn't been able to find her father's body. But the half-breed showed her, Pawkittew did, where the war-chief had put the pieces. It hadn't taken long for her to put events together: the war-chief, Tawnew, murdered and flayed her father, cut him up, before the ass-priest returned to resume his power, bringing He-for-whom-we-seek-life, bringing me to beget the new ass-priest of her tribe. Then she'd stabbed Tawnew;

his death so clear in her memory. She'd used the war-chief's body to patch her father's up, to restore his body. And she'd lain with me, hoping to conceive the promised child; she'd wished to take the future, the hope of her tribe on herself, to take the child she wasn't supposed to have into the mountains with Berrigan, all that old religion concentrated in her body.

Berrigan couldn't remember what their first time had been like, only that it had always been strange to be with her, that she'd seemed slippery, ungraspable as water, changing, like liquid shifting in currents under apparent stillness, like the pool where Legget had waited for Dutchess to come to him. He believed, as Sawpootway did, that she had always been waiting for him; though she'd married LeGuey and, he thought, been with me at least once, perhaps even the first night. Despite his suspicions when he found us at dawn, he believed she'd already, even in that betrayal, returned to him, as if he'd immediately become necessary in her life, the husband she'd expected after all, though she might resist. So she'd brought him back to her tribe, something to be displayed but never given, and he'd fallen ill there, so ill, sweating his body out in the Indian camp. He'd been surprised to live on, to elope with her to mountains, leaving his old life behind, even his only friend behind like the stolen gold he'd fought for. The British gold would be no use in the mountains; that world had begun to peel from him like a useless rind as he lay in his illness.

But he'd meant, at first, to leave the valley again. He remembered how he'd told her, his hands on her face under the first rough shelter he'd built and hadn't meant to last. She'd stood on tiptoe, and put her fingers in his; she raised his finger to her mouth, between her lips and teeth as if to silence herself. He didn't know why he'd felt so frightened; he'd attempted to withdraw, but she'd bitten to hold him, sucking his fingers hard, and he'd lost all desire to go. So he knew, through that fierce teasing; that she meant to stay, though she never said it outright; and he'd never intended to leave without her. The rind of his life didn't attract him enough, that world of white men she no longer cared for at all, or had cared for too much to return to.

Berrigan had built the new house to last, as Thurlow built now; and he thought once more, Sawpootway now silent beside him, that this life had been meant for them long before her old husband, LeGuey, had come and traded for her; had been meant when she'd lain in the hut of her puberty, waiting for the husband that hadn't come yet; meant even when she'd lain hidden by her parents as an infant, when they'd searched for her as if they didn't know where they'd just hidden her, as if they didn't even know that she'd been born to them. They took her like a present, from the bushes, then Berrigan believed she'd been his even before her parents discovered her, as if she'd been given to him in that interim, between her birth and discovery. As surely as he knew the valley had been meant for them, he knew they'd leave before long, at least for a time. He didn't know why they'd go; it was just what they would do, eventually. They would put it off until it seemed to come of itself.

Sawpootway's most recent silence, when she lay as if sleeping beside him, was like a balm in his ears, an assurance that his own dreams and memories were allowed him. Then he realized she'd asked him a question, speaking his name; he hadn't answered. He rolled toward her. "What did you say?"

At first she made no reply, except to move against him, to stroke his body, stretching her own as if to some special tension he'd need to match. He'd forgotten what they'd come to bed so early for. She didn't ask her previous question again, till he was about to enter. "When will he leave? When did he say?"

Berrigan withdrew, and leaned above her, supported by his elbow; but her own tension remained, her body poised on the edge of their act, held back only for that question. Berrigan said, "I don't know. He didn't say." He touched her breast tentatively. "Almost as soon as he gets back, I'd guess." She didn't move; yet her tense body still measured his length, as if she'd reached a sexual limit, or limit of despair over Dutch's departure. "They figured they'd get back late tomorrow. So a morning from tomorrow. I don't know; he might stay a few days yet." He almost wished he hadn't tried to answer honestly; a lie might have been better, any lie. He remembered again, as if it were something that might have particularly hurt her, that they'd found Dutchess's letter, announcing departure, under the covers of their bed. He wondered whether Adams had been the one to pin it there, so it wouldn't be discovered until they came to sleep or love.

She moved in invitation and he entered her quickly, renewed the customary, the familiar rite. Her body relaxed, became so soft from its former tension, as if she'd float, rise around his own body, taking his own dimensions as hers, her body enlarged to shelter his heavy bones. He weighed himself in that softness, and felt how near he was borne to earth, into a cave of rest.

Later, Sawpootway flung an arm over his neck, and her lips moved near his ear as if she'd speak a secret there, but he heard only the whisper of breath itself, coiled like smoke in his ear, then the even expulsion and return of her sleep, her breath bringing his own sleep on. He spread one hand on her belly and thought, now scarcely awake, that they'd always pretended the children couldn't hear them, always knowing children could, and Dutch and Dutchess had kept the pretense, lying soundlessly beyond the taut skin wall. The last sense Berrigan had before sleep was of the presence of children nearby.

He dreamed something he barely remembered later, of pale roses folding tiny men into them, to cover the men in sleep, the roses murmuring, like animals laughing gently, or like giddy women whispering their joy of love-making like honey into his ear, soft-tongued voices almost inaudible, the breath of the hidden animals. Berrigan himself peered out from the folds of a rose, and he saw his son's body before him like blue and white lightning, and that body struck down, a swift knife through the full length of the tree in the yard. The slash of light stood out clearly against the bark; then there was only the white scar in the tree, and no son remained, leaving that mark of his passage.

Berrigan woke to cockcrow in the false dawn; he rose up, silently, having seen Sawpootway wrapped snugly asleep in furs. He moved, through the cabin door, not into the new day, but into renewed full darkness on the porch. He wore only his nightshirt. He looked in vain for the light, the pale reddened horns on the mountain. Berrigan sat down on the porch edge. After a time, he became too cold, and he brought a fur wrap from the cabin, where Marie still slept, her face turned into her pillow. He sat on the edge of that porch and, until the true light peered through the clouds over the eastern mountain, he couldn't have said what he was thinking, not without great effort.

In the gray light, he stared at the cottonwood and saw, startled, a figure detach itself from the trunk, as though the bark had come away; and, though he'd thought the figure all imagination, he knew Dutch had been standing under the tree in darkness, watching his father. He knew the figure from the tree was Dutch, that figure arriving, placing one foot on the porch beside him. Yet he felt he couldn't speak till Dutch had.

Dutch said, "I couldn't wait. I couldn't stand to wait any longer."

Berrigan looked away, toward the tree, then toward the western end of the valley. "We weren't expecting you yet. Not till tomorrow." He tried hard to think what to say next. "Where's Thurlow?"

"His place." Though Thurlow's cabin wasn't finished yet, he'd been sleeping there, as Dutch had. "I couldn't sleep." He looked toward the cabin door, "Is she asleep?"

Berrigan said, "Yes, you'll wait."

They were silent, looking into the dull, cloud-covered dawn, until Dutch sat down on the porch. He said, "I wanted to hear again about the deaths. I want to sit here a while, and hear. I wasn't going just yet."

So Berrigan told him how the three men had once attacked him, for the gold he supposed, though LeGuey's motive might have also been his wife's betrayal; then how, with the half-breed, Drake or Pawkittew, he'd killed them; he'd found their bodies folded back on themselves, already dropping to earth, broken. He told and remembered how they'd looked in that death, as if trodden down, though LeGuey had lain differently somehow; all that time of violence inexplicable to him, as if it occurred outside of his life, as in a dream he didn't control. As he recalled it now, the half-breed had made peculiar signs, perhaps representing animals, upon the dead faces.

Dutch said, "And the other violence, the war?"

Berrigan shrugged, and did tell, briefly, how he'd been a volunteer, and of the long winter march through water on the Illinois prairie, when no one expected their coming, how they'd surprised the British fort at St. Vincents on the Wabash, above the Ohio. Berrigan felt what he said wasn't important to Dutch any more, or not very important: he was just trying to get events straight in his mind as if to confirm what he already knew. Berrigan also had to tell, without much detail, of the capture of the British pay wagon, the capture of gold before that long flooded march; and of a duel I once fought—I wasn't yet his friend— with the captain who insisted on dueling; then how we'd gone, Berrigan, me, the troopers Smith and Thomson, after the gold the three older ones had hidden with the captain, how Berrigan had then met Dutch's mother, found the gold, and carried it so far only to leave it, he supposed, to me.

Then Berrigan said, "Or you might find it still there, if you want it. Your mother could tell you how to get there." He thought a moment, "Or I'll tell if you want." Berrigan wanted to make a joke; for all these things he'd told the half-attentive Dutch, all that loosely narrated sequence of event, out of a now far past, seemed preposterous as told on the porch, in the poor light, as silly now as the deceitful plan Sawpootway had instructed her son in, the plan for Legget's deception. The notion had occurred to him that his own story deceived the son.

Dutch looked away to the east, his mouth compressed.

Berrigan asked, "Are you afraid?"

"Yes, I think so."

Berrigan said, "Don't worry about us."

SAWPOOTWAY STILL LAY IN BED, AND sometimes slept, in the coming of the gray dawn. She heard two voices on the porch. She dreamed two dreams, while voices intruded increasingly, until the speech of Berrigan and Dutch became too dominant, words risen to the face of dream, the voices, recognized, surfaced like creatures in water. She knew she was awake, and felt she'd been, in her recent sleep, curiously apart from her dreams, as if dreams became clothing that didn't fit her any more, the outworn images; she felt her body poised between two dreams and two voices.

She remembered a long dream of snakes writhing out of the dead bosom of a woman. She didn't think she knew the woman, though she might have when she dreamed her. A man she felt she did know, even later when wakened, but never could name, peered deeply into the holes the snakes made coming through earth. He was their father, but no snake himself. He existed in the pouring out of snakes from the earth, in the thaw of snakes. He glowed with increasing power; but ice formed on his brow. The female flesh melted around him, to flow past his legs like a river. He seemed to drown in that flood intentionally, as the snakes swam away hissing to each other, in the language only the snakes knew. When Sawpootway thought the man was Legget, he grew more like Thurlow; she was heartbroken, then embarrassed at such mistakes. She saw herself, in the dream, reviving him, and she felt she'd feed him her heart if she could, pressing his head to her breast. From his mouth, a small wolf with bent, gray ears emerged upon his chin like a tongue not fully formed. The man opened his eyes, and shrank from her, as if, startled to be awake with her, he'd leap back through his own heart, his flesh collapsing, his bones, undestroyed, surfacing like tree boughs on water.

She'd partially wakened, and heard something of the speech on the porch, fragments of the old story Berrigan was telling, and that story, in her interim state, had seemed fantastic until she'd remembered she'd been there herself, for most of the time of the old story, that she'd told their history to Dutch, over the years, in fragments similar to those she understood from her bed. As yet she hadn't thought it strange that Dutch was present on the porch; she'd recognized the voices, but hadn't named them. Husband and son, though heard, were almost anonymous.

As one dream became another, Sawpootway had thought the voice of Berrigan told its companion voice that Legget had come again, and she'd thought that was an impossible thing: Dutchess had gone; nothing was left for Legget. She was afraid Legget had come for her, not for Dutchess. Lapsing into dream she'd cried she was afraid of Legget's possible presence, even afraid of the porch voice's mention of that trapper. No one heard her cry. She felt it had all happened before, Legget's approach and this fear. In the bed, she'd covered her ears with her palms, so the sound of the voice's speech couldn't easily enter.

So she'd slept again and she'd dreamed of her sewing, the leather and the needles. In the dream, her hands covered her ears; if she put her hands upon the sewing in her lap, she'd have to listen to words about Legget. She reached for the sewing, needing its confirmation: a voice spoke of her existence in an old life. The voice said nothing of Legget; her sewing disappeared beneath her fingers, and she didn't miss it. Dutchess rose out of the water, lake water still and deep. The man, from her first dream, perhaps Legget, perhaps Thurlow, perhaps . . . The man from her first dream, a shape shifting, threw Dutchess into an oven, where, cooked, she became Sawpootway. In the oven, she bled forever from her womb, and no man would touch her. The man departed, betraying her as if he were one, now laughing at his joke, who'd already died, long before. The dreamer wondered if she was waking, through the laughter, to approaching voices. She felt still confined to the dream, as to the Indian oven, past and future elements of her sleep kissing in her shamefully, and she could see, though waking, no departure from the dream's ovenlike atmosphere, no new life or husband to change her fortune; and if she should escape from that initial confinement, she could see no further escape or departure, no release from the cold always forming above her, like a cap that a man's fingers pulled down, spread down to icy clothes or skin, a man promising rest, but lying, while she burned in her own body forever, unproductive, untransformed, while serpents brooded, waiting for her flesh, and a small wolf's white tongue roughly licked her lips and her tongue.

Berrigan's voice became clear to her, as if it had captured her dream, breaking oven and cold weather. Sawpootway struggled up with a power that surprised her; she came through the intricate webs of many spiders; she thought of the sewing she no longer did, and thought of his words, reaching like a garment to clothe her, as dreams had, words became something Berrigan wove to make them both intimate and distant, in a peculiar wholeness; though those words of his disguised some old argument between them. The dream faded, dissolved like a film that had covered her head, eyes, nose, ears, and was replaced by memory.

The scene she remembered was very clear: the twins returned from the creek, with cleaned trout Berrigan had caught, swung in a basket between them. The memory was so clear, and painful in retrospect, as though their departure was announced in that scene. She felt they freed her, unmercifully. She remembered the chickens had feasted on the remains of the fish, cleaning up the creek side, after the twins. Berrigan was afraid a chicken might get a little bone caught in the throat. Dutch held the fish out, and Berrigan inserted two fingers into the slit bodies of fish. The dark, cut bodies seemed to swallow all their rainbow light, to contain their light deeply, like something the fish no longer wished known to men; their bodies became dark pools they turned their lives about in, dying to that old world, swimming into themselves, to a new country where the death of fish would be natural.

Sawpootway still lay in bed at the coming of dawn and afterwards. Morning shadow fell over the house from the mountain, remainder of the greater darkness, the shadow like a sign upon her, a hand, reminder of her reluctance to wake, of her fear of waking: now her son would leave her. She realized, fully now, that he'd returned and talked on the porch with his father.

She wondered what she would say if she could speak to Legget again, through Berrigan's translation or in the trapper's language, speak over the water that rushed between them in the apparent stillness of the pool. The answers he gave seemed sincere enough now—about his family, about the woman he'd loved and who'd died. She wondered if he might persuade her now. She'd told Berrigan she'd seen Legget every night for years, in her dreams, appearing, disguised as her dead husband, coming back into her life. She'd said Berrigan had seen him too; but Berrigan always denied it. It seemed so unreasonable of him to deny it, and Legget's answers seemed unreasonable. Legget had refused to recognize himself.

Berrigan, though, had said Legget was somebody else. Then who was he? Who was Thurlow, who'd now moved into their valley, who intended, obviously, to make a permanent home? And who was this Adams she'd never seen, who'd taken her daughter? Dutch wouldn't go, she thought, if Dutchess hadn't. Who were these men to her, that they could affect her life? She listened for the voices on the porch, as if they might provide the answers, but Berrigan and Dutch couldn't be heard; they were silent.

Berrigan had already spoken of the old time of his life. Dutch's whole life intervened between that time and now. The father's history had gradually petered out; he remembered fewer details. Berrigan thought of Dutchess; she might return to the chickens, gathering the eggs, feeding them grain, or bearing water. For years the chickens had been hers to care for. Something had belonged peculiarly to each of them: to Sawpootway, the goats and the garden; to Berrigan, the fishing, the horses and hounds; to Dutch, the hunting since he'd been old enough. These duties became mixed between them, but Berrigan could identify those activities he most associated with each one. He could go on, if he chose to, combining activities to refute himself.

But it was Dutchess, as he looked at his son in the early light, who preoccupied him. He could only vaguely imagine her departure; for he'd forgotten how she might look rearriving, forgotten how he'd imagined her coming back to them, as if he'd never known his daughter's features. He stared hard at his son's face, to remember her—the strong nose and the wide mouth. He remembered her coloring was darker than Dutch's. Darkness spread, as if within, behind his eyes, until the reconstruction of her face, so carefully recovered from Dutch, was lost in her own darkness and disappearance.

He started to speak, but didn't; only the gesture, that would have accompanied speech, continued; his fingers described a long curving line through the morning's dull light, a path like the flight of the fish he'd once thrown to Legget, or like his children's smiles. There, in that motion, when he didn't speak, he felt he retained Dutchess. He'd have liked to speak of her then, to describe her in language, words of his mouth, to make somehow more permanent the feeling conveyed in the motion of his fingers.

Dutch watched him, expectantly, and Berrigan, embarrassed, hurriedly removed his hand from the air. When he looked at his son, he remembered how Dutch had held the basket of trout, still for probing by those same fingers, remembered that young man's body, which seemed even more piercing now, as if Dutch could walk through the trunks of trees, as through a cloud or through a mountain shower; all things divided to let him pass.

Berrigan remembered he'd removed his fingers from the trout, and taken the basket. He looked down at his son squatting on the grass; yet saw him, earlier, in memory, his solid back going around a corner of the cabin, as his sister had just gone before him, going for some unknown reason after her; then he saw himself, in the same scene, entering the house where the woman was cooking fish, her sewing spread like a cover on the table, as if sewing was what they'd eat on.

Words he'd say to Dutch now on the porch, words the silence between them seemed to demand, wouldn't come, wouldn't even begin to be said. In that other time, Berrigan had hung the net on the wall; Sawpootway had begun to cook something. He and Dutch both heard her in the house, muttering as if in prayer. Berrigan said, finding some words anyway, perhaps the right ones, "Your mother's awake." Dutch was already rising to enter the house; he nodded at the words his father said.

Berrigan walked to the woodpile. The chickens, noisy and tattered birds, seemed to call Dutchess to them; but Dutchess wasn't there. Berrigan remembered his children, young and shouting in the yard, playing with the long blue dogs. He cut into the wood and heard, between his strokes, the thin murmur of speech in the house.

Dutch wasn't long coming out. For a moment the young man watched his father work. Berrigan felt he didn't know the other, had never known, not even when he'd spread the small buttocks, cock and balls intimate with his fingers, when he'd made the child gasp and breathe. Dutch had always remained beyond his father, despite the violence of birth, far more than Dutchess, as if each male, to the other, was a part of the body forbidden to touch.

Dutch came forward and asked, "Do you remember the last time?" He said it as though the last time they'd cut wood together was both a joke and a secret they shared, something that affirmed the connection between father and son. He took the ax from his father. They split the wood, taking turns, as they had often. The grain, as though willingly, broke on itself under their strokes, under the blue lift and fall of honed metal, in the rhythm of the curved ash handle; each watched the other work the wood.

As if they'd planned it, slowly Berrigan's turn grew longer, so long at last no one swung the ax but Berrigan. Dutch had gone down to the cottonwood and gathered up his leather pack and gun; his father didn't watch him go.

Berrigan could hear the chickens, two hounds wrestling, snuffling noises Sawpootway made within the house. He heard a horse neigh down the valley, heard the stream go by, and the noise of the wood breaking under his ax. He thought Sawpootway might come out of the house. He swung his ax hard, and felt a peculiar freedom of arms; he sweated in an ecstasy of woodcutting.

He heard a sound and looked up, ax stuck in wood, thinking she'd come to join him. She hadn't yet and, when he looked around, he couldn't see any sign of Dutch. There was only Thurlow, who he'd all but forgotten existed, standing near the corner, frowning.

The preacher smiled and asked, "Shall I take a turn?"

She appeared in the doorway, an instant only, and Berrigan gave Thurlow the ax, though no wood needed cutting now; he went to her.

YET IT WAS ANOTHER SPRING BEFORE they left the valley, ascending past the twin-peaked mountain, and even then they probably wouldn't have gone, if Legget hadn't returned out of an early-spring snow storm; he brought them news of Dutchess's child. Departing, Berrigan felt a sense of reversal, like he'd felt years before, as though, while they climbed, events slid backwards through them, as if he descended into the valley and saw his young children playing among the long-bodied hounds, the thaw's course reversed; as if his children broke through a circle of hounds to welcome him, while their mother, under the small porch roof, stitched the leather of the shirt he wore in this departure, the last she made. In that shirt she'd illustrated him in terms of claws, shaggy heads, the dyed-white threads composing animals apparently all of bone, ponderous creatures that might stir, through dreams, into human lives.

They each led two horses. Berrigan looked back at her, between his animals, and saw her pull herself up a sudden incline, grasping a stiff shrub, picking her careful way; her horses lurched to keep up. Cinco and Spook ranged behind them. She still didn't seem to have aged, essentially, in all the years since they'd entered the valley; as if she'd the right to claim she'd eaten from the death of her old husband and of her father, becoming immortal. Berrigan had never believed she'd done that; he knew she hadn't eaten anything of

LeGuey, for only Berrigan and I had touched the little man after his death, to bury him.

Berrigan still thought it was the valley that kept her so, that there she'd entered that changeless life, amazing him, changing only in the fullness and the lightness of her flesh; yet now he felt that something terrible had, after all, happened in her life there, changes within her he alone had caused, as if all his acts and allowances somehow betrayed her, that he was unwillingly responsible for everything she endured: the birth, growth, and departure of two children, his own alternations of the flesh in sickness and health, seasons coming through him to hurt her. Yet it seemed to him now, in this ascent, that she'd retained throughout those seasons a great agility, transforming pain to a stillness in which she abided, fitting her shape, even her flesh, to the occasions, her slight changes of survival. The valley had allowed her that imperturbability at the core.

So Berrigan worried, superstitious, about leaving their valley. He feared, unreasonably, that her heart would be repulsed by the world they entered, her heavy bones softened in the waste. Her stitching had been so patient and attentive, as if the pattern were within her; she'd been absorbed in the task, careful for error. Now her face behind him was flushed full of her blood, in the difficulty of their climb.

That had been their life—the children sliding through the circling hounds like honed, swift knives, while she stitched the designs—but it was changed; for this whole year the children had been gone, and her stitching had disappeared from their house, after the shirt he wore. Berrigan felt the changes that saddened him again and, in nostalgia, he wondered what new things she might find of value in the world, dead to them so long, the world beyond the mountains. That time when they'd first entered the valley seemed close to him, when Sawpootway's body had swollen with the twins, so close he felt the time might return, as Legget had recently returned to the valley. And, he thought, if Legget can return with word of our grand-child, then Dutchess, as he'd thought, could come back to him, that she did come in his going out to her.

He wondered how her child was born: had her body fallen in ripeness, laborious in March? No, he was born before that. Did her boy child surprise her, pale from her dark body, blue-white like porcelain, a glazed child with a thin blue haze over his eyes? Did her own body compel the birth, when her will seemed not her own will any more, urged by the doctor's fingers? Had Legget said she had a doctor, or some woman, or Adams, or Legget with her? Berrigan couldn't remember: the fierce image of the child's birth confused him. Had contractions been so terrible, and the boy upside down, and did the doctor cut her to ease the child's exit? Had her son breathed from the first and pleased her with that release of his breath? Or did she see, worried, the small toes thrust toward the eyes, the contorted child the doctor or midwife had yet to surprise into life, as he'd once star-tled Dutch?

Berrigan could still feel his son's contraction on his smallest finger, when Dutch gasped his first breath and learned life in the cold morning air. Berrigan could hear again the double rhythm of the living breath, pulse and repulse. Did Dutchess's body go as pale in the birth as the child's body? Irrelevantly, for the first time in years, Berrigan remembered how red

Dutch had actually been at birth, as if rubbed raw; his paleness came later, after much sleep. That time, when his children had lain in Sawpootway's arms, when mother and children slept and Berrigan pressed his fingers into the wax of the stubby candles, seemed as near to him now as his family had then seemed far away in their sleep. Now Legget had already come, in long past February, to tell of the grandchild's birth.

Berrigan had risen in darkness to the knocking, and stared, when he saw who'd come, till Sawpootway said, "Let him in. The man will freeze out there." Thurlow, who'd come for dinner, stood up. Legget muttered in the cold, words about Dutchess that Berrigan couldn't catch. Legget sat and shook before the fire. In his disbelief, Berrigan was silent, full of so many questions he couldn't formulate yet. Then Legget withdrew a letter from his clothing and, after Sawpootway took it from his hand, he lay down by the fire and slept two days; Sawpootway changed his clothing and treated his skin, toes nearly frozen, fingers stiff, cared for the cold man as she would a child. The letter told of the child's birth.

Only Sawpootway and Thurlow were with him when he woke. The storm ended the night Legget came and Berrigan, insisting Thurlow remain with Sawpootway, had gone a second time to look for Legget's mule. Sawpootway had decided Legget should be wakened, and forced to eat as he had been once before; she gave him broth in a cup, and he'd swallowed it, but seemed incapable of speech and slept again. She wanted to hear his voice, telling anything of Dutchess or Dutch. She squatted at the fire where a pot hung. It was Thurlow's voice she heard, in sound squeezed from the throat, saying, "He's awake!" When she turned, Legget had seen her. He scrambled to his feet as if Thurlow and Sawpootway had caught him in an act he was ashamed of. He stared at Thurlow, who told him who he was and then sat down on the bed's edge.

Sawpootway said, "Sit down there. You must eat before you speak." For Legget did seem to be trying to say something. She got him broth, while he sat in her old chair, and stood before him, as if to make sure he ate.

Twice Legget paused, from eating. Once to ask, "Where's Berrigan?" Then again, "The boy, where's the boy?" He stared, suspiciously, at Thurlow, as if it were that other man, the stranger, he questioned.

Sawpootway answered the first question, but only turned away at the second, toward the fire.

Legget finished his broth. "That mule's dead," he told her. While she took the cup to refill it, he added, "Figured I'd be too."

After the fourth cup, and a bit of meat, he didn't want any more. Sawpootway sat in Berrigan's chair, studying him. He didn't seem to be the same man she'd seen before, barely recognizable from one year to the next. "Tell me," she said. Thurlow leaned forward, sharp elbows on his knees, sharp chin in his palms; he was slightly uncomfortable, for Legget kept glancing toward him, still wondering how this strange man had become so at home in that house, so familiar with the Indian woman.

He told Sawpootway, "I was there. It went pretty hard, before her time, you see. Adams, he was out on some business, down to the Ohio." He didn't explain how he'd heard of their presence and sought Adams out, found him at a livestock sale, among the traders and trappers and hunters, the various animals. He didn't say he'd only come to their house after the child's birth. It was almost three months later he'd admit he'd lied, and plead for their forgiveness.

As Legget told of the hard labor, Sawpootway moved her hands slowly on her knees; she'd soothe her daughter's absent, struggling body, to ease the birth, midwife to her own grandchild. She saw the young woman's eyes enlarge, the forehead shine. The child appeared to her, small, dark as his mother.

Legget said, "It changed her so, like she was somebody else when she saw that boy in her hands. She was a lot like you then." He paused, wondering whether to say what he thought he'd say next, "Before it come out, she thought it was a girl." He laughed harshly, as though he forced the sound and would choke on it. "She wouldn't believe it till she'd touched him, till she'd felt how he was a boy."

Sawpootway asked, "There was a white doctor there? He did it?"

"Sure, I wouldn't have got something else."

Sawpootway felt she wanted to hold that child, to comfort the small male against breasts full of milk, to let their bodies assume a common rhythm. In Berrigan's chair, she swayed slightly from side to side. She would sing to the boy, an old lullaby of her tribe, one she'd just remembered; she swayed in its rhythm. She opened her eyes and found Legget staring at her. When she'd cared for cold Legget, during his sleep, she had thought how she'd treat her grandchild; she'd removed the trapper's clothes, and he'd slept like the dead while she washed him and laid him by the fire wrapped in warm furs. She felt so tender toward him, for he'd come in difficult weather, the uncertain season, swiftly in a very long journey, to bring news of her grandson. She felt tender even though once in that sleep he'd angrily called Dutch's name; then he'd wiped the sweat from his forehead and eyes, as though a spider web obscured his vision. Sometimes he'd opened his eyes, but slept on as she bent above him. Thurlow was there all the time, and remained, speaking little, just a presence in the cabin. She heard Legget's strained laugh again.

He said, "I've not been well, you know. There was a fever all the early winter."

Sawpootway was surprised to hear Thurlow speak; so was Legget. "You had a hard time coming. I'm sure they're grateful." The former preacher blushed. "Look, you can stay with me here, till you're well. I could use some help, come spring."

Legget stared at the other man as if he hadn't heard him.

"You can stay," Sawpootway said.

Again Legget rasped out that laugh. "You know," he said, "it embarrassed me. To be there, after the kid came. I guess I kind of surprised the doctor, 'cause I was backing toward the door, and I'd got my hands out, like this, like I was trying to push them all away." He held his palms out, first to Sawpootway, then to Thurlow, and said, toward the latter, "You see, that doctor thought I was the father. He did."

Sawpootway dished out herb and meat stew for them all.

"You know," Legget said, "you really did me a lot of good. I don't think I loved her at all. How could I? I didn't even know her, did I?" He laughed again, a slight, soft laugh, as if meant to be heard only by himself, a laugh he was trying out on them. "Yes, I think you did me a lot of good. It was some kind of madness, wasn't it?" He said, "I guess Dutch got back all right." When there was no reply, he said, loudly, looking up, "I didn't mean him any harm."

Sawpootway still didn't say anything, but Thurlow came to his feet and said, "He got back all right. He got back," as if it was his duty to console Legget. Sawpootway rose and went behind the skin wall. The men sat uncomfortably; they heard her weeping softly. The two men made some small talk, about the news from the world, talk that didn't interest them that moment.

When Berrigan arrived, Legget was asleep in the chair, arms up to cover his face, his fists tight like a child's. Thurlow had covered the other man with furs, and was preparing to hike, through the diminished storm, to his own, now completed, cabin.

When Berrigan's astonishment at the scene was gone, and he'd questioned Legget, after peeking into the children's room to find Sawpootway sleeping, he got himself some stew from the pot and watched Legget in sleep, as he ate. Thurlow remained, after they'd laid Legget on the bed, as if uncertain whether Berrigan wanted him for questions any more. Berrigan said, after one of the long silences that had come to them, "Well, at least he saw Dutchess. That's what he said he wanted." Then, repeating an earlier question, "But he hasn't seen Dutch? He doesn't know where Dutch is?"

Thurlow shook his head, "No." He sat forward in Sawpootway's chair now.

Berrigan felt he knew the spirit of the messenger's sleep, as if he could peer into dreams. He asked Thurlow, "What's the child's name?"

Thurlow said, surprised, "Why, I don't know."

"He never said, and she didn't ask him?"

Thurlow shook his head. "He did most of the talking; he just didn't say." He looked at Legget on the bed, and suggested, "We could wake him."

Berrigan laughed and said, "No, it can wait."

Now, in the middle of May, Berrigan and Sawpootway passed into sight of the river. The child's name was Orcus; no one had been surprised. They came where Berrigan had met Legget the year before. The trapper remained in the cabin behind them, in the valley with Thurlow, like a son they trusted without evidence. They knew now he'd lied to them about his presence at the birth, and knew he'd come through difficulty to bring the news. He had emerged from that long sleep peaceful and full of a life they'd not expected; he was active and kindly about the place, with no sign of bitterness, eager to help them in their valley lives. He reminded them of an old friend they'd once left behind, despite his difference. They didn't mind nearly as much as he did that he'd lied about his role in the grandchild's birth.

Now they were gone, Berrigan imagined him, tending to things as the family had, for they'd seen him help with the animals as if they were his own; and they'd seen him, recently, with a long stick, poking bean holes; for Berrigan and Thurlow and Legget worked the ground, after snow melted late, with the wooden plow. Legget hadn't seemed very sad to see them go; he stood absorbed in the valley. Berrigan wondered if Legget dreamed, ever, of Dutchess, as he worked where she'd worked before him. Thurlow and he would trap and hunt.

Berrigan had told no date when he thought they'd return. They'd stop to see Sawpootway's people on the plains, though she didn't believe they'd find them anywhere; then they'd halt briefly for the grandchild and daughter and son-in-law, listening for word of Dutch; then they might go to Pennsylvania to see if his parents still lived. They might never return.

They led their four horses down to the river, and the two hounds followed. They came toward the pine tree above the river bend and saw the roots rising from the earth, and saw the fanned, green needles above their heads, and branches spotty with cones. They decided to rest there. They approached the shade of the tree tentatively, as if that cool shadow might dissolve too soon, as if the tree, the trunk, if touched too hastily, might slip through their fingers, their grasp, and carry them back into a former time.

Legget wouldn't leave their concern yet; as though they still feared him. Berrigan had recently said, "He seems so innocent, after all," and it was that they emphasized now, his innocence remaining behind in the valley, as if underground until they'd return, until some new life had been prepared for him, in the chrysalis or by the thorn.

They thought of Legget lying dormant, while the ex-preacher guarded the congregation of one, guarded a Legget, who expected nothing of his life any more, holding to something like innocence. At least it seemed innocence to them; it was the only word either had said to describe their impression of Legget in the valley with Thurlow. Yet they knew he wasn't innocent, and they recalled his invented tale of fear concerning their grandchild, how he'd tried to ward them off, mother and child.

Legget and Thurlow had stood together to watch Sawpootway and Berrigan go. Legget hung back, near a patch of vanishing snow. Thurlow came close to Sawpootway. He'd said, "Everything will be fine here.

Don't hurry back on that account. Take time for a good visit." He'd looked to Legget as if to have his words confirmed, and the other did seem to nod in agreement, and did smile as if embarrassed. Sawpootway leaned toward Thurlow from her horse, her body inclined through the cottonwood's shadow. She touched Thurlow's face with her hand, and looked toward Legget, including him in the farewell. Soon, Berrigan had said, "He seemed so innocent, don't you think? Did you see how he smiled, shy as a kid? He seems so innocent, after all."

SAWPOOTWAY BELIEVED THEY MUST gather their lives. They lingered in that place, by the pooled river, where they'd met Legget for talk the previous spring, and they'd linger in other places; for, despite the outward movement of this journey, the breaking away from one place, from the continuous round, they'd entered a time of stillness in their lives. She sat by the roots and peered over the water, abstracted, like a spirit revisiting the past scene. It surprised her that this place had no greater hold on her than it did; there was a connection still, definitely, but it was as though she lay, like the meat of a nut, now loose in the old shell. The vital connection seemed to be prepared somewhere else, in the future of her life with Berrigan. Even her children seemed less attached to her life, as they moved in their own, newly discovered lives, beyond their parents; she suffered their going like a pain that had passed without knowing.

They would move toward her tribe in the plains; but she didn't believe they'd find the tribe. She felt they'd disappeared, all of her people, vanished long ago, as if it was true they'd gone into her own body; her children had become for her, unconsciously, through an old obsession about their origins, the last members of her people, and her children had gone from her body and from the valley, into the world. She wouldn't examine that feeling. She thought if they did find anyone they'd only be a bedraggled, starving remnant, hanging on to gods they no longer believed in, a remnant incapable of regeneration, old men and women without any offspring, who would not speak of the ass-priest, Pawkittew, nor of the new one who might have been born, even if ass-priests existed any more (the old gone into the promised exile, and the young one, who she believed never born, gone to seek a white person to bring into the tribe as Pawkittew had brought me once, brought the one they'd called Fish-out-of-water and He-for-whom-we-seek-life). She would find, by the lake on the plains, only the dead-in-life the tribe had become for her, the old ones of her own clan still lecherous but infertile, their war-chief long dead in battle or wasted without spirit.

That scene by the lake, northeast of this river, where they'd left the gold, would not contain her either, whatever she found there, though she would perhaps linger too long. And she wouldn't, she thought, returning there, be able to understand what madness once led her to kill the war-chief, revenging her father, nor why she lay down with me, to conceive a child another of her tribe was chosen to bear. Her desire to revenge her father's death and her desire for such a strange child had passed, finally, she thought, as if into the stitched designs she no longer practiced, those desires no longer a part of her active life. She felt she'd almost forgotten that her children might not be Berrigan's; she'd come to assume they were his, because he assumed it. She felt, by the river, that she was becoming a newer, freer person, someone gleaming, shedding the dead life. The notion, thought explicitly, seemed silly.

Sawpootway looked at the stream that swept below her, that was full of the mountain's debris, and she felt that the mountain, dissolving and rushing away, would bear her and Berrigan on. Above her head, the snowline receded toward the twin peaks, as it did every spring, unveiling the black, wet face that descended beneath the cap; this spring it seemed to her an inhuman face, or an old face, of her own, almost unrecognizable now.

They lingered, hesitant to go a mile upstream to cross the river, to descend again past the present site and pass beyond the bend: she knew the twin mountain peaks would remain in her sight for miles, each time she looked back, like a reminder of their mountain past. She watched Berrigan, who seemed strange to her, as if she'd just discovered he was someone she hadn't known; he became, in this beginning of their journey, a surprise to her. He seemed unpredictable. He stood still above her as she crouched at the tree. In the thin, high air, her body strained in the new emotion, as if it would transcend its own pulse, to assume the rhythm of the river's flow down the mountain, as if her blood pooled within extended boundaries, inclined toward that future she couldn't yet imagine, the future of their bodies moving together beyond mountains, down to plains, to prairies.

She'd closed her eyes, then was startled she'd done so. What she saw then was Orcus Berrigan, the father of her departed children, walking out to stand waistdeep in the water, as if to test the hidden current where the flooding water pooled over old banks before the wild rush to the bend, Orcus Berrigan beneath the pine tree's outstretched boughs. She was aware of the horses standing quiet beside her as she watched him, as if horses were as attentive as she was. She couldn't understand what he was doing. The hounds joined him, Cinco and Spook, the blue hounds damp and swimming, noses flat against the water, necks tensed. She saw him bend down to the water until his fingers seemed to tangle in the flow, as in a woman's veil, Orcus Berrigan with his catch of dripping water as he stood again, his face turned toward the sky in the east.

He seemed abstracted, his mind far from the scene; but his figure, in the water, was clear and concrete in her mind: there he seemed to swell, becoming fuller, in his brown skins, his body more powerful; and his head loomed from the gray goat-fleeced collar, his bare head like a brown, shaggy thunderhead that overlooked all her own concerns. She was frightened: in this beginning of their journey, he grew huge to her, as if he were a flower that, shrunken and faded, had bloomed again beyond any previous growth. Then that mood broke and, though still strange and unpredictable, he became more like the Berrigan she'd known.

He bent or squatted slightly, half submerged, as the hounds plunged around him in their joy. He played with them, calling their names, "Cinco! Spook!" He clapped his hands at the dogs and pretended he'd catch them by the long tails floating behind their swimming bodies; he flung water as though he'd catch them in strands of the river. The hounds, stretching taut necks farther, swam away and returned near him, as if he controlled them with threads of the water spun from his hands, threads of elusive colors in the sunlight, in the game with hounds. The image of the sun was shattered by their movements in the pool; Berrigan broke and handled the sun, transforming the scene as if to make it over to their future lives. Then he straightened, that single sharp gesture of the whole body ending the game in the water, and she saw his eyes on hers, and she would have asked him what he thought he was doing there, but couldn't, as if his eyes, turned on her so suddenly, held her tongue as still as the horses beside her.

Then she realized the horses weren't quiet, and that Berrigan was looking, now, at the mountain, not at her. Squatting near the black roots, near the horses, whose unshod hooves she heard on the rock, she too looked again at the mountain they'd come beyond, upward toward the high peaks thawing, and she thought of their valley, and the men left there. Who were those men, Thurlow and Legget? She expected no answer even from herself.

Orcus Berrigan opened the mountain and she discovered him in that act. When she looked toward him again, he'd risen, walking toward the tree, as she felt the mountain flow into their journey, bearing the valley along. And she thought how this was the place Legget had come for her girl, but Dutchess had been hidden from him, as though in the pine tree, out of his reach. Berrigan climbed toward the shore; he must come up so far to her, to the roots of the tree, as those black roots seemed to swell from an underground treetop.

She felt light then, as though her body had ascended out of the earth; as though Berrigan climbed to follow her up among the black roots and the horses, drawn by her ties to him, by their mutual ligaments, and she was wreathed by the roots and horses, on top of the earth roots, while the horses rose above her head like the tree. She felt the earth was drawn into the tree after her, and she might sit, together with Berrigan, high above, as on a bough, while the sun prided itself like a rooster above them. They would shut their eyes while the clouds swarmed about them.

She closed her eyes and pressed a pine cone, hard, into her palm; she would give that to Berrigan to press, and his hand would take the shape, as hers did, of the imprinted cone. She would hold him in her arms, as if her arms were all that protected him from a long fall down. She opened her eyes. Berrigan still stood in the water, no closer than he'd been before. He watched the dogs, swimming out of the water before him, shaking the water out of their hair; the spray from their bodies touched her face.

She stood and called his name, "Orcus Berrigan!" She couldn't remember the last time she'd spoken those words. He looked at her, waiting for her to continue. He would be strange to hold now, chilled by the river. Surprised at her own, so sudden outcry, she squatted down, and wrapped herself again in her arms.

ORCUS BERRIGAN HEARD HIS FULL NAME and he saw the woman squat down, her huddled body on the shore; he thought he must speak to her. He didn't know what to say, so said what had been in his mind just before. "You know, who'd have thought Legget would come again? This winter, I mean." She looked at his eyes, but didn't answer. He wondered what else he could say; he was worried about her, about the tightness of her arms around her body. He looked toward the twin peaks and then at the black rock below like an old face he felt a tenderness for, the face of someone like his wife or one of his children. Now the valley beyond the mountain sheltered Legget and Thurlow. "Like they were its treasure," he said. "Like Legget and Thurlow were the ones." When she didn't ask what he meant, he changed the subject; "Are you still so against him, against Legget?" He smiled broadly, to make sure she saw he teased.

She shook her head and, to his surprise, she asked, "Are you against me?"

Berrigan did seem, even to himself, so solid in contrast with the fluid of the river flowing away between his legs, set somehow apart from her, in opposition to her trembling form on the shore, as if he were able to go more certainly than she could, in the direction the river took, into the life before them; yet he felt able to carry her with him, in that rhythm he felt in water at his thighs. He said, "No, I was never against you." He almost said more; he didn't know what. She glanced toward the pine top and smiled, slightly, as if in wry disappointment, as if something had gone from the tree, something she expected to find.

She asked, "Do you think she sounded happy?"

"Who?"

"Dutchess, in the letter she sent us."

He frowned and nodded. "Why not? She was happy enough to go. We'll see her now, for ourselves. The child too." He thought she looked at him so greedily, as though she hadn't seen him before, as though they'd been so intimate before that moment she hadn't been able to see him. She seemed embarrassed to stare so hard at him, and she looked down at her toes and the roots of the tree. Berrigan felt very strong, felt he could lift her and bear her through the pool to the other shore, and it would be good to take her on his shoulders; in the deep water she would lie flat on his back, as he ferried her over.

Sawpootway said, "Aren't you against me, for what I've done?"

"You think that? You don't know me then. Then I'm not who you think I am." Berrigan still frowned as he spoke, furrows deepening with each phrase in intense concentration.

"No," she said, "I know you well. Too well, I think."

"I don't understand."

"There was a terror from my past. Too much reminders of old deaths. My husband. My father."

Berrigan felt guilty, as if he were responsible for both deaths she mentioned, instead of one; but the guilt he felt seemed false to him now, like a hat that didn't quite fit, like a buffalo hat he'd worn years before. He felt, even in that guilt, almost free from an old bondage. With pleasure now, he thought of Thurlow and Legget: if necessary, those two would wait a long time, becalmed in the valley. If he wished, he could stand in this water and speak to Sawpootway forever: Legget and Thurlow would remain, until they'd departed and returned, the two men become, Berrigan thought, more constant than anyone had ever planned. Legget was almost like a child of his own; and he now could think better of Thurlow than he could at first, clearer and more kindly, more trusting of the preacher he'd found when he came home with Dutch. Then Thurlow had seemed all worn out, from a long and terrible journey, an old, collapsed figure nobody would ever listen to again, with nothing left in himself, after his great kindness to Sawpootway, after bringing her home through her madness. Now Thurlow seemed so full of his own health and usefulness in the valley that Berrigan had recently, after Legget's return, asked what had brought him so far from any church. Thurlow hadn't seemed reluctant to talk; but his answer didn't help Berrigan understand much. The preacher, or ex-preacher, had said, as though it explained all, "Nothing. I just kept riding farther. Then the mule died, or the horse; I don't remember any more. And I walked. Then I found her, or she found me. What else can I say?" Much more, he could say much more, Berrigan thought.

Sawpootway said, "I'm glad Legget came, that other time. For Dutchess."

"Why?"

She said, "Do you think what happened was bad to happen? Now do you think it was?"

Berrigan studied her. She was steadier now than just before, as if she was surer of him. She didn't even seem uncomfortable under his stare, and didn't seem to expect any answer to her question. He thought the question had just been talk to cover her, something to touch him with, as she watched him cooling from the heat of the noon. Berrigan felt the cold water rush through his thighs, around his firmly planted legs. White water, around a rock, leaped toward his belly; he liked the pressure of the flood against him, and the compactness of his cock and balls so recently emerged from cold water. He thought he might make love to her then, but let the thought pass.

He thought of the few white men who came into these mountains, to their valley; all were renegades, he knew, in some way. He imagined Legget sitting under the small porch roof of Thurlow's new cabin, two hounds beside him, as the preacher came out the door. The three hunters—Marais, Cantrieux, Azul—approached on their horses, waving their blue guns in threat or greeting. The notion occurred to Berrigan that they were looking for Adams, who'd been one of them. Legget's mouth was closed and stayed closed, but his eyes widened and he laid a hand on Hasty, the hound on his right; Thurlow stopped near the door and carefully watched. Then the two men at the cabin showed obvious relief to find the three horsemen came only to ask for food and water; they didn't come dangerously, after something they'd lost. They made a camp, and almost ignored Thurlow and Legget, in their own concerns, as if they now moved in another kind of life, like angels or fish. Berrigan, imagining those men, could almost hear their surprised, lowered voices speaking of the emptiness of the other cabin. He was drawn back, again, by Sawpootway's voice.

She said, "Will we camp here?"

Berrigan didn't care: what should they hurry for? Her presence startled him, as her voice had, out of the imagined scene in the valley. "Might as well go on, while it's light," he said; for there was nothing to keep them there. "Or stay, if you like." He was walking toward the land. He was tired of the water, and couldn't understand why he'd stayed there so long. He was afraid to stand off any longer from the shore, afraid that, lost in his imagination, she'd fall vague in his mind, even in contrast with visions that were like the water and air, as if the connection between them, if he didn't go to her, might become unreal, too tenuous to hold, and they would slip away, each from each, as if they weren't meant to remind each other, constantly, of themselves.

Under the pine tree, near the dark roots, near the horses and Sawpootway, Berrigan stepped, and the water receded down his body, swiftly, as his feet cleared the river, and he lunged up the slight inclination of the earth, past the hounds. Now she was a clear figure before him, and he felt he'd brought some new strength to them from the water, and some grace he'd learned there, the new ease of one both ponderous and sure. He said, "We'll eat before we go. Are you hungry?" As he looked at her, he felt something moved from him, some issue from his body to hers, as if he offered himself from his hands, as though his fingers became elongated, flying bodies that, in passage, connected the sunlight and the water, something like his fingers moving between them with the rhythm of his lungs. He felt they could go the way they needed; as if, in his fingers, the spirit of the mountain's thaw came from him, something like a pulse that neared her on each alternate beat, and fell back only to slip closer, each long beat like a spark achieving a new freedom and repose, cleaving the interval between them.

Her own spirit seemed to rush into the air to meet his spirit or whatever came from him. She approached and seemed to enter her own most natural medium, and he thought she must feel relieved, as a fish might falling into the water after a leap through the foreign air. She seemed to come, as he did, where breathing could be easier; so he touched her, and felt her body soften, thawing from the old life; his arms held her loosely. Berrigan wondered how his wetness felt to her belly and below. He felt she would lose nothing of him. She'd ease whatever fall he fell, catching up whatever issue came from him, ease his descending flow, as if that were her ultimate test, the last thing she was called to do: Berrigan felt she wouldn't, willingly, let anything fall from his flesh.

Then he released her, and stepped back; and her fingers closed on the air where he'd stood. He had thought of their food, and went to their packs. He knew she watched his back move to the horses, watched his hands on the straps. When he turned, she was sitting on a rock. He brought the smoked meat back.

She said, "Yes, I am hungry. Aren't you?" She stood up and turned to the rock; there was dust on the stone. He had already seen the marks of her fingers, when he'd come from the horses. He saw what she was looking at: the wide imprint of her buttocks in the dust, the two parts shaped to one print of her body contained in the cloth. He thought of who might come and see her mark; she didn't dust anything off. Berrigan said, "This afternoon we could catch some trout here, if you want." She turned from the rock and took some meat from his hands, and the hounds came up, hungry after swimming, drying in the sun.

ON A HOT AFTERNOON IN LATE MAY, far from the valley, far from the stream, and from the lake and the plains where her parents found none of the old tribe, in a humid place between two great rivers, Dutchess knelt on a blanket, in the grass by her child. For Dutchess, in those days, the world was almost wordless, as if she lived in a cloud of silence, humid off the rivers. The hens, she thought, came up to stare and cluck in wonder at the small pink animal who shared the world that had no human language.

Dutchess meant to teach the child to sit up, with her help; she wanted his fingers to seize, as they had before, on her two fingers. The child closed his eyes, and clenched his fingers only on themselves, like soft fat petals into his own palm; but she didn't mind that closing; she knew she could open the tiny fists at will, or wait, like she did: she had all the time and the boy belonged to her.

Meanwhile she muttered his name, repeating, for her own ears, not even for his, "Orcus, Orcus, Orcus, Orcus," as if the sound were his body, and again she thought the boy overheard and smiled to his name or to her voice alone. That name didn't sound like her father's name at all, but like the name of a flower, an open flower, not these hard flowers, these small closed fists of the child. She didn't know her mood, in that afternoon, was changing. She thought the name was the child's name, and she asked herself if the name had ever been her father's.

She'd never called her father that name; it was not his name any more: the name was of the boy or a flower. She felt heavier than she had a moment before, her bones too weighty in her flesh, her whole body too pulled down to the child as if he hung, still unknown, in the intimacy of her womb. She touched his face, and wiped his nose gently, as though her fingers probed a wound of her own. The child glanced up at her then as though he kept a secret, and he did wound her within, where he'd once grown, in the place where her blood was his not five months ago.

Her mood *had* changed toward him; she only then knew it. His wide eyes seemed, in that one brief glance, almost inhuman to her, revealing nothing of the child she thought she knew, only the emphatic strangeness, of something she was forbidden to know;

but she felt she could almost express that strangeness, though the boy child seemed so perfectly at one with his breath, with his own interior rhythm, that he could never, after all, have been any part of her body.

Dutchess wished the child could speak to her, in that painful moment when he seemed most indifferent to her desires; she wished he could name what he knew within the closed beat of his heart. She was awed by him, as she hadn't been so strongly before, as if she learned she'd given birth to a god. She remembered the intimacy she'd felt when she'd named him, how near child and name and she had seemed, in an intricate relation. Impatiently, she probed the small fists; but the child's grip was always stronger than she thought. Then he seemed never to have had anything to do with her body, and she was moved to reassure herself she was still bound to the boy.

He had been a winter child: two rivers had frozen and men walked from one shore to another shore. She'd lain in a darkness like her blood. She'd been torn in her pains, hopeful only for the last pain that would thrust the child into the world; between contractions she lay in wait for the next pain as if she'd surprise her hurt. The doctor and her husband had been all but invisible to her, vague forms near her feet and her head, thick posts meant to mark boundaries of her labor, while she learned to live in the pain of the child and in the hope of pain. Their voices had been alien voices as if angels or animals spoke beyond any concern with her.

She'd been so pleased, before, when Adams promised her a real doctor; she'd looked forward to his coming almost as much as she'd looked forward to the child. Yet she didn't care about the doctor after all: it was the pain that took her. She didn't fight: she lay in wait, then let pain have her, till all she knew was pain and waiting for pain; and even the child seemed forgotten, in the purity of her isolation: her body didn't belong to anyone else; she knew it as her own body.

Dutchess brought the baby from herself with little help from the doctor. The high, thin voice pierced her darkness but didn't startle; for hers hadn't been, after all, the darkness of unconsciousness. She saw the boy dangle upside down, and the doctor smiled with a smile she thought false. She felt Adams's hands on her head, and heard his voice, rising clearer, saying all was well with her. She was afraid the doctor wouldn't give her the child, but he did; she named him out of that intimacy of pain. She'd slept, pleased with her body, as she'd never been so much.

Now she watched to see if the name she'd given confirmed itself in the child, to know if she'd named him the right name. She knew she was bound to the child, but her heart was wary of a kind of fierceness she felt in him, in the closure of his fingers, like petals at dusk that would force themselves inward to hardness like a fruit. Her teeth nipped her lip as she strained, slightly, to unbend the boy's hands, but she didn't, after all, seem to have enough strength; she couldn't get the proper grip on his hands, and she didn't want to apply more force. And she wanted them open, did not want only to raise the child by his arms or fists. Her heart insisted that he open to her, to be raised up by his own grip on her fingers. Then let his fingers close as hard as now, when her fingers were well within hers. While she still pried, she hadn't ceased to wonder at her son.

He began to wail. She let his hands go, and wept quietly. When his own cries became more subdued, he turned his head to one side as if he listened carefully to her weeping, her sound so soft only she and the child could possibly hear it. Let him, she told herself, only release his grip on himself, and enter her dream of him; let him lean into her now only, then it would be forever.

Dutchess listened to their weeping, their sounds mingled, and she felt there *was* something like words between them, as if they both spoke, in a pre-human language, in what had become their single voice, as they'd once had the single body. She felt he was also aware of that common rhythm of their lungs and hearts, as if their breath and pulse, in expulsion of tears and of air, returned in gasps, combined to something like words, within their difference, her own pain the alteration of his; so her tears and his became comfortable to Dutchess, and she didn't try any more to pry the small fists.

Between them now, as their tears eased away, she knew they'd established a new relation between them, old like some familiar tale she'd heard as a child. She became so aware of their breath she felt she couldn't breathe without the child. The idea pleased her, and she touched his hands: they would open in their own time, soon now, and her child would sit up.

Dutchess wiped both their faces with the hem of her dress; she gazed over the heads of the chickens that went about their own business. The tears left a mist, like a thin membrane. She looked toward the growing town that was still little more than a rendez-vous where two rivers happened to concur, a meeting place for traders and trappers. She saw, through the misted eyes, two shapes approaching like trees, over the yard. The chickens parted, and she recognized her husband; she didn't think she knew the other man.

Yet the other's body, straight and sure in walking, passed, familiar, through air and chickens, through her own veiled vision. She saw his smile, wide beneath the hat brim. She took the baby up in her arms and stood, unamazed, to see her brother, the hard, diamond-like body she thought should cut through her heart with an expected pain.

But there was no pain at all, only the casual greeting between them of kiss and embrace she scarcely noticed; she continued to exist in her previous condition, with her son, as if she and Dutch were distant and indifferent relatives meeting after many years. She heard him say he couldn't make up his mind to come before, that he'd trapped on the Missouri and wintered near the Lakes. Her brother meant no more to her, less, than Legget had, who'd also come with Adams, one day just after the child's birth. She felt she existed beyond her brother now, it didn't worry her: she was bound to her child, wherever her child was bound. She was bound in the relation, reconfirmed today, she'd first known in the pulse of pain and waiting, in the contraction and release of childbirth.

She was aware of her existence even beyond her husband: he'd come into the void for her once, when no one else approached, other than family; but the child came, and that was her religion, found in birth, there the ligaments that held her in life. She was grateful to Adams, for the way he stood, even now, above her, large and protecting; she thought there might be another way to love him again sometime, but not today. Now he was the comforting shadow upon her and upon the child who slept in her arms. She didn't need Adams for much today, only his familiarity, the warm darkness, and she needed her brother less than Adams, if at all. She almost said so, but didn't want to speak, in that mood, any more than necessary. They weren't twins or, if they were, that didn't seem important in her. As they went into the small, carefully whitewashed house, Adams asked, as if it was something he'd forgotten till now, whether their mother and father had come with Dutch; but the question didn't really interest her. Her parents, like her brother, would be too much intruders.

They all sat down in the house, Dutchess on the floor, and Dutch began telling how he'd left their parents, how their parents had been. He kept talking to her, and she'd nod, and even speak if necessary; but she wasn't in their talk; her brother soon spoke more to Adams than to his sister. The child woke, and she fed him, her breast bared to the lips and gums of Orcus; she smiled up, as though permanently, into the shadow of her husband.

They were all smiling as if they agreed with each other. She even became more aware of her brother's mouth, when he was silent, wide and closed, lip on lip, like a flower. Then she was sad, under his smile, knowing, in memory, their relation, how he was her brother: he seemed far into his own life, as the child was, as she was into the life of the child.

Again her mood was changing. But she felt protective, defensive about the boy in Dutch's presence, as if the child that now lay belching against her shoulder were a secret, sex still unknown, she must protect in her womb. When her brother accidentally caught her eye, while talking to Adams, her look startled him, as if out of an indifference of his own. She thought he recognized her then as she saw herself. Still his body seemed too hard and foreign to her, not like Adams's familiar power in softness. In the present scene, her husband had drawn back into his darkness, as if he wouldn't intrude between brother and sister any more than between mother and son; he became, she thought, a cloud of patience behind their heads.

She moved over the floor of the single room with young Orcus, while the men watched her. There wasn't much anyone could find to say any more. She placed her sleeping child in the softness of his cradle. Now his small hands lay open, the fat fingers pliant. She squatted to watch him. She could open and close his fingers anytime she wanted; yet she didn't touch him. She wanted him awake, only then to feel his fingers close tightly on her own as she raised him. She felt as patient as Adams, as though she could wait on anything now; the child and Adams taught her.

Dutch came and bent down toward the bedding. Dutchess realized he hadn't looked closely at the child before, as if, knowing her fears, he'd held back on purpose. She shrank from him, as his hand came down to the baby. To her surprise, she touched his hand as his fingers lay on Orcus's forehead; and she felt no danger in him, only a connection, out of their childhood, between her and her brother, as if they at last acknowledged a secret they'd held together.

Dutch removed his fingers from the baby, and held her own hand when they stood. Adams moved from his chair and came close behind her. She could feel his presence over her shoulder, like a touch she hadn't noticed until it was withdrawn. Dutch released her hand, and she peered down at Orcus, whose small features rose as though from deep water she and Adams and Dutch passed over like rain clouds. She thought she could feel the physical formation of words in her mouth, prompted by combinations of things in the afternoon. Those words would provide her entry into another world than the one she'd lived in recently;

she didn't even care what words might come; they could even be something she didn't understand, like the babblings of a baby.

She studied the child's face intently, as if it were writing she must decipher or lose her life, the test for her continuance. The men spoke of what Dutch planned to do, but their talk was soft, not meant to intrude upon her thoughts, nor to wake her child. "No," she said, and could almost see her brother shaking his head before she asked, "Won't you stay with us?"

A Note on the Design of This Book

The text of this book was set by Fototronic CRT in a type face known as
Garamond. Its design is based on letterforms originally created
by Claude Garamond, 1510–61. Garamond was a pupil
of Geoffroy Tory and may have patterned his letterforms
on Venetian models. To this day, the type face that bears his name
is one of the most attractive used in book composition,
and the intervening years have caused it
to lose little of its freshness or beauty.

Composed, printed, and bound by
The Colonial Press Inc., Clinton, Massachusetts
Typography based on
a design by Elton Robinson

Cover illustration by James Grashow
Photograph on back cover by Morris Dressler
Cover design by R. D. Scudellari